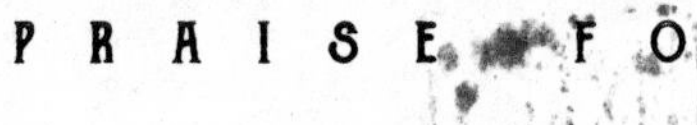

"A dark, fantastical, and, at times, chilling story.
Rue Morgue Magazine

"As Andersen has done for the book's beautifully bizarre yet detailed illustrations, Ford has filled his novel with customs and side stories—some no more than a sentence or two—that make the world feel real, wonderful, and horrifying simultaneously. And though in many ways it seems nothing like one, this novel is at heart a fairy tale in the grand, dark tradition of the best of such stories....In this moving and magical literary journey, a heroine grapples with a terrifying power."
Kirkus Reviews

"The last thing I thought would happen to me when I read this novel was cry: not once, but several times—the kind of tears that make you put down the pages, press your hands against your face, and sob like a child. *Lily* is the heart-breaking story of a lonely young girl and a curious old woman, of their reluctant and hesitant, then breathtaking and courageous, journeys into the women they were destined to become. It is a fairy tale that takes place in the magical world, in the real world, and within themselves—at once terrifying, sorrowful, and triumphant, revealing the wondrous mysteries of life and death through exquisite prose and illustrations. *Lily* is a masterpiece."
Livia Llewellyn, author of *Engines of Desire* and *Furnace*

"Such gorgeous imagery throughout this novel—both in the stark beauty of the story and in the illustrations that accompany it. *Lily* is atmospheric, gothic, magical, touching, and haunted, with moments of suspense and terror, like a dream mixed with a nightmare. Lily makes me think of Stephen King's troubled young misfits and the heartbreaking heroines in the fairy tales of Hans Christian Andersen."
Timothy Schaffert, author of *The Swan Gondola* and *The Coffins of Little Hope*

"This is one of those books in which the story is so strange it reads rather like a dream you once had. And the writing is so good, you forget you're even reading. You don't read *Lily*—it projects itself into your soul, in flickering chiaroscuro, smudgy and sparkly at the same time, like Staven Andersen's wonderful illustrations. The novel is unnerving and gorgeous. I love the quiet heroism of Lily, the girl who can foretell anyone's death. And the sordid awfulness of the revivalist circus and its born-again clowns. Most of all I adored the grisly, shrieking nastiness of this incarnation of Baba Yaga."
Paul Magrs, author of The Adventures of Brenda and Effie series and *Lost on Mars*

LETHE PRESS

[M]ichael Thomas Ford

Lily

Illustrated by
Staven Andersen

Published by Lethe Press
118 Heritage Ave, Maple Shade, NJ 08052
lethepressbooks.com

ISBN:
Paperback 9781590212684
Hardcover Deluxe: 9781590210888

Cover Art and Interior Illustration: Staven Andersen

Interior Design: Inkspiral Design

For Tove Jansson,
who answered my letters

• ONE •

On the morning of her thirteenth birthday, Lily kissed her father and knew he would be dead by nightfall. The image of his death dropped into her mind without warning. As her lips touched his she saw behind the thin skin of her closed eyes his face, pale and wet, rising up from the waves surrounded by caressing fingers of sea grass, and she screamed.

Her mother started, and the pitcher of milk she held in her hands crashed to the kitchen floor, where it exploded in a fury of glass and spread over the boards. Her father grabbed Lily and put his arms around her, but she beat her hands against his back, sobbing and trying to push away the lifeless body that slumped on her breast.

"Lily, what's happened?" he asked.

Lily looked into her father's anxious face, at the blue eyes clouded over with worry for her. She opened her mouth to speak, and found that she couldn't. Her voice seemed to have been drained away, and as hard as she tried, she could coax no sound from her empty throat.

"What's the matter, my darling?" her father pleaded. "Are you all right?"

Lily nodded. She knew that she was in no way all right, that nothing was all right, yet she sensed that to indicate otherwise would somehow throw everything even further out of balance. Her father clutched her to his chest, and again she saw his body hovering in the blue-green water, the eyes wide and staring, the mouth filled with the sea. She struggled to keep from retching, putting her arms around her father's neck, relieved to find that his shirt was crisp and dry under her fingertips.

"Why don't you go upstairs and lie down," her father said, stroking her hair softly. "Then this afternoon we can open your presents."

Lily nodded and turned away quickly before his skin could once more become wet and his lips swollen. She ran up the stairs to her bedroom and shut the door behind her. Lying on her bed, she put her hands over her face and waited for the vision of her father's death to come again. When it didn't, she fell into a troubled sleep and began to dream.

The branches were dead, thin and pale as bird bones and iced with frost. As she made her way through the trees, her bare feet left small hollows in the snow, which the edge of her night dress filled in behind her, leaving no trace of her passing.

She was unaware of the cold that kissed and nipped at her bare skin. She moved across the snowy ground as if it were summer grass, pushing her way through the empty arms of the trees until the forest opened up before her and she was standing in a clearing. The trees formed a perfect circle around her, their branches closely knotted together. Above the circle in the wood the moon hung low in the winter sky.

Sitting in the clearing was a cottage. It looked like many of the cottages in the village, with a pointed roof and small, square windows whose glass glimmered silvery in the moonlight. Tendrils of smoke crept from the top of the stone chimney, and through one of the windows Lily could see the pale yellow light of what she was sure must be a fire. She felt the cold of the snow for the first time. She shivered, and drew her arms around herself. Beneath her bare feet, the cold crunched and bit at her toes.

She walked to the door of the cottage and knocked. When there was no answer, she put her hand on the latch and lifted. The door opened, and she went inside, shutting it behind her. The warmth of a fire greeted her, and she felt the cold slipping from her skin.

Standing near the hearth was an old woman, stirring a cauldron that hung over the fire. Her long hair fell about her face in knotted tangles, and she was humming to herself a song that sounded to Lily both wild and soothing at the same time.

"I'm sorry to intrude, grandmother," Lily said. "I knocked, but no one came."

"I heard you," the woman said, turning her face to Lily. Her eyes were black as the new moon, and her nose so long that it nearly touched her chin. Her mouth held a row of crooked teeth, and around her throat was a necklace of bones. Lily was startled by her appearance, but said nothing.

"You have come to Baba Yaga's house for something," the old woman said. "What is it?"

"I — I don't know," said Lily. "I found myself here."

"No one finds herself at Baba's house." The old woman tsked. "The path is too well hidden. You come here only when you are ready to be tested. Are you ready, child?"

Baba stopped stirring the pot and came toward Lily. Lily backed away. She did not like the look of the old woman's gnarled hands, each finger ending in a broken nail.

"Are you ready?" Baba Yaga asked again. This time, her voice was cold.

Lily could only shake her head. She didn't know what Baba Yaga meant. Ready for what? How had she come to be there?

"This is just a dream." Lily held up her hands in front of her face.

Baba Yaga laughed, filling the small house with her shrieks. Her voice rattled the window glass. On the hearth the fire died down to a frightened glow. "No one dreams in Baba's house. Answer me, girl."

Baba Yaga appeared right in front of Lily. Lightless eyes stared into Lily's face. She could smell the old woman's stale breath, ripe with the scent of mouldering leaves. She trembled, trying to still the racing of her heart.

"Ready for what?" she whispered.

"For the riddles," Baba Yaga said, turning her head to the side and grinning. "Baba asks, and you answer. If you answer correctly, I give you a gift."

"What kind of gift?"

"A birthday gift," answered the old woman. "It is your birthday, is it not?"

Lily nodded. "How did you know?"

Baba Yaga cackled, spinning around in circles until she was twirling so quickly that she became a blur. When she came to a stop, she was near the hearth once more, stirring the cauldron. "Baba knows much," she said.

"And if I guess wrong?" Lily asked. Now that Baba Yaga was some distance from her, she felt a little more brave.

Baba turned and grinned. One long finger reached into her maw of a mouth and stroked a jagged tooth. "Then I eat you," she said.

Lily looked at the necklace of bones around Baba Yaga's neck. Now she understood their meaning. Her heart turned cold, and her breath swept out of her throat in a gasp. Baba saw her fear, and smiled. She laid aside the long spoon she stirred with and came back to where Lily stood, frozen in terror.

"A fair game, I think," she said as she waited for Lily to speak. "Now, are you ready, girl?" She reached out one bony hand and took Lily's fingers in it. As her claws curled around Lily's soft hand, the girl gasped.

"Are you death or life?" she asked.

Baba Yaga frowned. Her eyes hardened, but she said nothing.

"I see nothing," Lily said. She looked at Baba Yaga's hand in her own. "I see no ending for you. Why is that so?"

Baba Yaga dropped Lily's hand and backed away. "It is Baba who asks the questions," she said, her voice like grinding millstones.

"Tell me," Lily pleaded. "Why is it that I see no death for you?"

"Silence!" Baba roared. She grew larger, filling the house until her head was crooked beneath the rafters. Her black eyes blazed with cold starfire, and Lily trembled.

"You are not ready for Baba's game," the old woman snarled through teeth the size of axes. "Now leave this house before I decide to eat you anyway."

"Please," said Lily. "I need to know what I am. I know you can tell me."

"I will tell you nothing. Go before I lose my temper."

Her hand swept through the air, the force of it blowing Lily toward the door, which opened by itself. Lily shielded her eyes from the wind, and felt herself being pushed through the doorway and into the night.

She tumbled into the snow and lay there, the cold soaking into her skin.

When she looked up, she saw that the clearing had changed. Now it was surrounded by a fence of pointed sticks. Atop each stick sat an empty skull with pale light shining from its eyes. Lily gazed at them in horror, then looked into the gaping door of Baba Yaga's cottage, which now stood on two huge chicken feet. Through the blackness she saw one of Baba's gigantic unblinking eyes watching her.

"Go," said Baba, her voice pouring from the windows and the chimney. "And do not come back until you are ready. The next time I will not be so kind."

Lily staggered to her feet and ran. She pushed open the gate in the fence of skulls and fled into the forest. Her hands pushed at the branches, and her feet slipped on the frozen ground. The snow fell fast, grew thick, and the wind whipped it about her in gusts that stung her eyes with cold. There was no path for her to follow back to where she had come from, and she groped wildly in the blizzard for something that would lead her to safety.

She looked up at the moon, and saw to her horror that it was the dark, cold eye of Baba Yaga looking down at her. The winter night broke open in a terrible smile, and the stars sank into the hungry mouth of teeth.

"Are you ready?" came the haunting cry. "Are you ready, girl?"

Lily collapsed into the snow and cried. As the blizzard swept over her shaking body, she wept, and the tears froze on her cheeks.

She awoke with a start, looking up into the white expanse of her bedroom ceiling. The quilt was pulled up around her neck, and the room was filled with an oppressive heat. There was a sharp crack of light, and then came the sound of thunder rolling across the sea. Lily looked to the window and saw that outside the sky had turned the ugly yellow color of fear.

She glanced at the clock and saw that its hands held the time at late afternoon. She had slept all day. She remembered little of her dream, but she recalled clearly her vision from the morning. Her father would be out at sea in his boat. As she realized this, the rain swept in from the swells and began to pound on the roof.

The sound drove her out of bed and sent her stumbling for the door. As the terror of the morning rushed back and filled her mind once more, she was overcome by the need to find her father, to hold him in her arms and feel the life flowing in him again. She fumbled with the latch on her door, struggling to remember what his face looked like. When she couldn't, her heart jumped crazily.

Her nightgown grabbed at her feet, tripping her up as she raced down the set of twisting stairs to the kitchen. The storm outside rocked the world as she reached the bottom and ran into the kitchen calling out, "Father? Where is father?" Her voice was unfamiliar to her, as though she were calling into the wind and was hearing her words echoed back in tatters.

Once in the kitchen, she stopped. Her mother stood near the stove, her arms wrapped protectively about her chest as she rocked silently against the wall. "Where is he?"

"He's dead," her mother said into the silence, the words slipping out cold as well water. She looked up at Lily, and Lily saw that her eyes were empty. Lily didn't know why, but she understood that anger had settled into her mother's heart.

"He's dead," she said again. "Drowned."

"Where is he?" Lily demanded, and when no one answered her, she screamed the question again, her voice shredding the quiet. "Where is he?"

"The body is on the beach," her mother said.

Lily ran to the door. Her mother made no move to stop her, turning her face away. Outside, the wind and rain swarmed about Lily like bees, stinging her skin and blinding her eyes as she made her way through the clouds of sea lavender and down the path to the beach. From the crest of the hill she could see the small crowd gathered at the water's edge, and she made her way toward it, the sand rough against her bare feet.

Reaching the beach, she pushed through the crowd of onlookers, the women, men, and children of the village who had come as soon as they'd heard that the sea had taken one of their own back into her arms. Lily knew them all, but at that moment she recognized no one as she looked past them to the body lying on the sand. Her father lay there, still, as if for some unexplained reason he had fallen asleep in his clothes, while around him three men stood helplessly.

Seeing Lily, the crowd stepped back as Lily fell to her knees beside her father. They watched as she reached out and ran her hands over his face, the skin mottled in bursts of plum and rose where the sea had kissed the life from his lungs. Lily brushed the seaweed from his dark hair, and her fingers danced over his closed eyes. Her long black hair fell in curls over his chest as she bent her head and wept into her hands.

"It's time to take him back now, child," said a kind voice close to her ear. She looked up into the face of Alex Henry. The closest thing the village had to a doctor, Alex Henry knew the ways of life and death not because he'd studied them, but because he'd lived them many times over. He had delivered Lily, and her father before her, and his father before him. There were some who believed he was as old as the land itself, and even the oldest among them could not recall a time when he had not inhabited the small cottage at the very end of the point that stretched furthest into the sea of any piece of land along the coast.

Of all the village, only Lily's mother had not entered the world cradled in Alex Henry's hands. She had not been born into their midst, but brought to it by Lily's father, who fell in love with her during his one venture outside the familiar walls of his life and returned with a thin gold ring around his finger and a woman who feared the sound of waves against the rocks.

Slowly, Lily rose to her feet. Although she hated to leave her father, she knew that Alex Henry and the others would do what was needed. She left her father there with them and returned to the house. Her mother said nothing when she entered the kitchen, and Lily did not speak to her.

She went upstairs and into the small bath. Its windows opened out over the rolling seas, and because the house was built on a cliff, she could see no land below her. She often shut the door and stood looking out at the endless plain of water. Caught up there between sky and water, she sometimes played that she was a maiden who peered through castle windows day and night, watching for her lover to return from a voyage across the seas, his arms laden with strangely-scented flowers.

But now things had changed. She was no longer a maiden. She was just a girl, a girl imprisoned in a single thin tower that rose up from the sea like a great needle piercing the world, and from which there was neither entrance nor escape. She was a girl who held death in her hands, gazing out her window onto the lifeless bodies of those who, driven mad with desire, had tried to reach her by throwing themselves into the sea. She saw love bruised on the faces that looked up to her window, and she cried.

She cried for a long time, thinking of her father and how she had killed him. She looked at her hands, twisted into balls in her lap, and she felt evil in them. She felt it running through her veins, and she hated it. She wanted nothing more than to reach inside her chest and pull out her heart, beating wildly, and throw it into the sea as an offering in exchange for her father's life.

She stepped out of her nightgown, moving to stand in front of the long mirror her father had hung on the wall nearest the sink. Her body was thin, the skin slipping lightly over bones. Her dark hair fell loosely about her shoulders, and she saw for the first time that her breasts were becoming those of a woman, that the small patch of hair between her legs had thickened. She saw reflected in the clear face of the glass the shade of a beautiful girl who was not her.

It was this girl, she told herself, who had killed her father. In crossing over the line of her thirteenth year, which brought with it the swelling of her breasts and the unfolding of her body, she had unknowingly awakened some deep magic that needed for its working the sacrifice of love. It had reached out and taken greedily the thing she loved best, feeding itself on his soul.

Lily hated this girl, and as she looked at her image in the mirror, she determined to stop her entrance into the world. She turned to the bath and drew the water. It tumbled hotly into her hands, and she welcomed the heat as it drew itself into her skin and banished the chill that had invaded her bones. She lowered herself into the comforting curve of the tub and let herself sink into the water as it rose to surround her. She closed her eyes, imagining herself floating in the sea. The water rose over her hips, then surged around her breasts, and still she kept her eyes shut. It licked at her throat, and then she felt it close over her mouth and nose.

Only then did she open her eyes, gazing up through the thin skin of water that covered her body. She could see the familiar shapes of the bathroom around her, thrown out of focus by the distortion of the water's motion. She wondered if this was what it was like to drown, if just before death the drowning person looked up and saw through the waves the shapes of a familiar world stretched into fantastical lines. She wondered what her father saw just before the water filled his lungs and his heart had stopped beating.

The water became deeper, filling up the big tub until she was lying at the bottom with a foot of ever-shifting golden light between her and life. There, caught between the worlds of water and air, she floated, listening. Her ears were filled with the sounds of the storm coming from far away, as though somewhere above her a giant blacksmith was beating his hammer against a forge and the echo was rolling down and around her head, becoming less powerful as it pushed its way through the water until, reaching her, it had become a soothing pulse.

Without wanting to, she found herself thinking about the ability of water to shut out the harshness of the upper world. She recalled once when she was very small being on the deck of a boat during a sudden and furious storm, and looking down into the black waves. The shrieking of the wind and the startled cries of the other passengers had upset her. Then the boat had shifted violently as a wave lifted it up, and she had been dumped into the ocean. The blackness closed over her head, and as she sank into it, in the moments before someone dove in to bring her back, her one thought had been not how frightened she was, but how quiet and calm it had been under the water.

It was like that now. Outside the storm raged, while in the tiny bathroom at the top of the house on the cliff, a girl who was not yet a woman was rocked in a warm cocoon. The shifting light threw patterns against the porcelain so delicate that the slightest movement of a finger or toe caused them to fall apart like breaking glass, only to reform moments later in entirely new ways as they played across her skin. She felt as though she was a creature waiting for its time to be born, knowing that while it remained in its shell of light it would be forever protected.

After a minute had passed, her chest began to ache, as the oxygen she had drawn into her lungs at the last moment before she submerged ran out. Her body cried out for her to leave the water and return to the realm of air. At the same time, she felt a peculiar desire to stay where she was, to let the water drag her even further down into itself, where she would not have to hear the sounds of storms. She wondered how many people, when they drowned, faced an instant when they had to choose to keep reaching for air and life or to simply sink. How many of them, thinking they wanted nothing more than to draw breath once more, stopped only inches away from the surface and, bewitched by the quiet, turned back. She imagined her father trying to push his way up through the blue as the remaining oxygen within him evaporated into his blood. She pictured him frozen, knowing that another pull of his arms would bring him through the barrier between life and death. She wondered if he'd had to choose.

Then came the moment when she herself had to make that decision. She could lift her head and rise up, or she could remain still. Despite the burning of her lungs as they called to her for air, she felt something comforting about the idea of taking the water into herself, of filling up every empty space inside with warmth. She closed her eyes, surrounding herself with the feeling of it. And as she did, she saw again her father's face, the dead eyes staring into her own, and she chose.

She screamed, the sound emerging as bubbles that rolled out of her mouth and went speeding up to the light. Her body followed, her head rushing up behind the scream until she was through and air was filling her lungs in great gasping sobs.

• TWO •

ABA YAGA NIBBLED the last bit of meat from the finger bone, then sucked on the end, pulling the still-hot marrow into her mouth with a satisfying slurp. She dropped the bone into the bowl on the table, and reached for another. Finding the pan empty, she uttered a curse and pushed the bowl away. She tried to remember if there was another child in the cellar; she didn't want to kill one of her fine, fat chickens.

She was always ravenous when awakened from a deep sleep, and her mood was not improved by the dream she'd had. The girl who had come to her was unlike any she had ever encountered. Filled with wild magic. The question was, how would she use her power? The possibilities were many, and Baba considered them all one by one. Such a girl could be very useful. Or dangerous. Probably both.

Her stomach rumbled, and she got to her feet. She walked down the seven stairs to the cellar door and peered through the tiny window set into the wood.

"Is anyone in there?" she called, rapping on the door with a bony knuckle. It was difficult to see in the dark, and the shadows played tricks on her eyes.

A whimpering sound came from one corner. "Please." A boy's voice. "Let me out. I promise I'll be good."

Baba Yaga's spirits brightened. She wouldn't have to wring a chicken's neck, or waste time plucking feathers while her stomach grumbled. "Come on, come on," she said, opening the door. "Make yourself useful."

The boy scurried out. Standing before her, he trembled. He was small and thin. His face was dirty, and there were bits of straw in his hair. *A bit like a chicken himself,* Baba Yaga thought. She wished he were bigger, or that there were two of him.

"Are you afraid?" she asked.

The boy nodded his head.

Baba Yaga tried to remember what he had done to land himself in her cellar. Stolen an egg from her henhouse? Taken the wrong path through the forest? Accepted a dare from a friend to knock at her door? Perhaps he'd simply decided to see if the stories were true.

Unfortunately for him, they were.

Grabbing the boy by the wrist, she dragged him behind her as she returned to the kitchen. Her hunger was reaching monstrous proportions, and she considered eating him uncooked. But the taste of the roasted marrow was still on her tongue, and so she opened the door to the huge oven and threw him inside. She hummed loudly to drown out the sounds of his protests, but these lasted only a few moments. Her fire was hot, and soon the cottage was quiet again.

She settled into her chair to wait. Again her thoughts returned to the girl. It was seldom that she found herself intrigued by anyone, particularly a human. But this girl made her curious. *Curious enough to leave the forest?* she asked herself.

She hadn't had such a thought in many a year. Now that she did, she considered the question. Was it time for an adventure? What could she gain from it? Perhaps nothing. But it might amuse her to see where this child went and what she did. *And it's not as if you're doing anything else,* she reminded herself.

The smell of roasting meat filled the air. She sniffed, inhaling deeply, and her mouth watered. Yes, perhaps it was indeed time for an adventure. But first, a bit of supper.

• THREE •

N THE WAY OF THE village, they buried Lily's father that evening, despite the storm that continued to rage around the point where the cemetery had stood since the first inhabitant had died and been laid to rest there, looking out over the sea, her grave swept clean by endless winds. It was there that the people gathered at dusk, the lanterns they held in their hands casting a golden pale over the hole that had been dug

as soon as news of the drowning had spread. Beside the hole lay the body, wrapped from head to toe in whitest linen and tied around the chest with a red cord.

The village had no priest, as they followed nothing that would be called a religion by anyone who happened upon them murmuring into the waves before launching their boats or saw them pinning small bags of salt or bunches of mistletoe inside the pockets of their greatcoats before setting out after dark had fallen. Yet they were possessed of rituals as dark and as strong as any performed by the servants of God, and it was Alex Henry who led them through them. He stood now beside the mouth in the earth, looking out at the sea and waiting. When the last of the sun had fallen behind the horizon and the first and brightest star of evening was visible even through the cloud-washed sky, he turned to the assembled villagers.

"It is time," he said, and nodded to the two men on either side of him. Moving silently, they took the head and feet of the body that lay on the grass and gently lowered it into the ground. Then they stepped back, and all eyes turned to Lily, who stood at the opposite end of the grave from Alex Henry. Her mother had refused to come, locking herself in her bedroom when they came for her, and so she stood alone looking down at her father's shell.

"It is the child who begins it," said Alex Henry, and Lily walked to the pile of earth beside the grave and took a handful of dirt. Clutched in her fist, it was cool with rain, and she felt it compress into a ball as she squeezed it tightly. Turning to the open hole, she held her hand over her father's chest and crumbled the earth in her fingers. It fell in a fine rain over the linen, dusting the body as cinnamon might be sprinkled over freshly-baked bread. When her hand was empty, she turned away.

One by one, the villagers filed past the grave, each one taking up a handful of earth and passing it over the body of Lily's father. This much of the death ritual they shared with those outside their world;

even the children understood the importance of covering the body with earth from their hands. Lily watched as fathers led to the grave little ones barely able to walk and helped them cast their offerings into the darkness.

When they had all passed, Alex Henry nodded once more to the two men beside him, and they began to fill the remainder of the hole, their shovels working like clockwork arms as one lifted a spoonful of dirt, turned it into the hole, and then swept away as his companion echoed the sequence. Lily knew that they would be done quickly, as tradition demanded, and that before the moon rose to its highest point her father would be wrapped in earth.

The villagers began the walk back to the small group of houses, and as the last person passed by her, Lily fell into step with the others. Moments later, the song of death began, the first high keening note sung by the woman with the most beautiful voice. The others joined in after her, and soon the night air was filled with the sounds of many voices. Lily sang too, taking comfort in the words of light and love and renewal. Her heart was sore, and she knew that she would cry more tears in the days to come, but as she watched the procession of gentle light wind its way down the sloping path and into the welcoming arms of the village, she sang with joy.

They came to the doors of the Great Hall, and went inside. As they did at each death, they would spend the night together, eating and drinking around the fire. The youngest would be told stories of the creatures that came out with the moon and of things that danced beneath the sea. They would hear of the fair folk and the selkies, of the White Ladies and the kobold. They would be told of Foolish Sarah, who followed a man with the feet of a goat into the forest and returned seven years later, her mind half gone, and of the young man who listened too closely to the promises of a vodyanoy and was drowned for want of a kiss.

Like the funeral, this was the way of the village. Lily could remember with great clarity the first time she'd sat in the hall, on a winter's night when the sea wind hurled snow sharp as knives and they gathered to celebrate the death of old Elsbeth Applegrim, almost two hundred years old when she'd turned from her baking and crumbled into dust on the kitchen floor. Lily had sat, eyes wide with terror and excited wonder, as Alex Henry had told the children why the villagers wrapped their dead about with red cord.

"The soul," he said in a voice like whiskey seeping from its cask, "is tied to the body like a lover to a lover. When one dies, the other wanders alone and afraid. We bind the soul to the body so that it remains at sleep. If we did not, the world would be crowded with souls looking for their missing selves."

Lily had seen ghosts. Everyone had. They appeared at moonfall and in the hours afterwards, pale forms that walked the fields and peered in windows. In general they were stupid creatures and not to be feared, but Lily knew that sometimes they gathered someone who looked like their missing selves into their arms and carried them into the next world. They did it for love, that was understood, but still their touch could bring death.

Sitting by the fire and looking into the dancing flames, she thought about the red cord wrapped tightly about her father's chest. She imagined digging through the earth and cutting it, freeing his soul so that she could see once more what he looked like in motion. But she knew also that it would bring pain. Years ago, a young man had done exactly that, sneaking away from the safety of the Great Hall to the cemetery and unearthing the body of the girl he'd loved. Her spirit had risen, and he'd reached out to her, only to feel the life taken from him as she reached cold hands into his chest to warm them.

The flames blew hot breath over Lily's skin, and the voices of the people talking around her provided a soothing murmur upon which she let her tired body rest. She thought about her mother, locked in the bedroom of the empty house. She pictured her huddled against the wall of the bedroom, staring at the bolted door and fearing any knock that might come against it. She wondered if her mother would open the door should her father's wraith come calling for her, or if she would put a pillow over her head and scream until morning drove him away. Her mother did not believe in such things, she knew, but she also knew that belief had little to do with whether a thing was true or not.

She was woken from her half-sleep by the touch of Alex Henry's hand on her shoulder. "I have something for you," he said, handing her two packages wrapped in paper and tied with string.

Lily looked at the bundles, turning them over in her hands. "What are they?" she asked.

"Your father's birthday gifts to you," he said. "I brought them from the house."

Alex Henry walked away and rejoined the children waiting for him to tell them another story about Black Hannah or the silver-eyed foxes that darted beneath the fir trees on Midsummer Eve carrying messages between the worlds. The other villagers were busy about the Hall, tending the roasting meats, sewing, and remembering other nights like this one.

Lily picked up the larger of the two packages. It was surprisingly heavy. As her fingers worked at the knotted string, she imagined her father wrapping it, his big hands deftly knotting the thin twine as though he were mending a tear in one of his nets. Even more clearly than she remembered his face, she could recall the look and feel of his hands, so often had he held her close or lifted her up, laughing, and spun her around until the sky and sea melted together and she felt the pounding of the earth's heart in her own. His hands with their long fingers, the skin cracked from pulling the rough nets into the boat and from lifting heavy tangles of fish, flapping and dripping, from the ocean.

The knot came free, and the string fell away from the package. Lily tucked it into the pocket of her dress before pulling apart the paper to see what lay beneath. It was a hand mirror, a small round of polished glass set in a silver frame. It looked old, like something that would sit on the dressing table of a very rich woman, for her to hold in her hand and look into as she fixed her hair or applied color to her lips. Lily wondered where it had come from.

Lily picked up the mirror. The metal grew warm in her hand. She traced her finger over the silverwork, the seahorses and outlines of crashing waves decorating the back, feeling the ridges and valleys beneath her fingers. It was one of the most beautiful things she had ever seen. The edge of the frame was also worked up into waves of silver, and falling crests of water framed her reflection. She looked at herself, and was surprised to see that the glass reflected nothing of the room behind her. Only her face was visible, and no matter how she turned the mirror, she saw nothing else. The glass itself was very old, its surface thin as paper. Yet within it her features were shown perfectly, as though her mirror image were even more alive than she herself was. This disturbed her, and she turned the mirror over in her lap and picked up the second parcel.

The smaller gift turned out to be a small wooden box. It was perfectly smooth, with no inscription or design marring the deep red skin of the wood. Nor were there any hinges or locks; the top was carved to fit perfectly over the bottom. Lily lifted the lid and found inside a seashell. It was unlike any she had ever seen before, perfectly round and large enough to cover the whole of her palm. It was pale blue in color, and its surface was swirled with violet, like the color of the clouds just after a rain. She picked it up, and found that its sides curved back under itself, forming a hollow shape. Around the sides were tiny holes that created intricate patterns all around the edge.

Also inside the box was a note. Lily picked it up and unfolded it. Written in her father's clear, fine hand was a short letter.

Dear Lily,

I found this shell many years ago, when I was the age that you are now. I have never seen another like it, just as I have never seen another like you. As is so with other shells, when you listen to this one you will hear the sea. But sometimes you will hear much more. I took it with me when I left the village, and when I needed to return its sound led me back.

Always remember that I love you.

Lily folded the note with great care and slipped it back in the box. Then she lifted the shell to her ear and listened. The sound of the sea roared through its emptiness, carrying with it the sharp cries of gulls, the slap of waves, and the whistling of the wind where it sang freely while tossing the waves into the air. She had heard these sounds many times echoed in the hollow of a shell. But somehow this shell contained not an echo but the true voice of the sea captured within its glossy walls. She put it too back into the box and replaced the lid.

It was nearing midnight, and the villagers were gathering in the center of the Hall to dance. The frenetic movement of hands and feet, they knew, kept away anything that might wish them harm. The rush of bodies moving about the room was sure to create a circle of love and warmth into which nothing dark could pass. And in movement and dance and laughter, they were reminded that they were alive, that their arms and legs could still respond to the sounds of fiddle, flute, and bells.

Joining the others, Lily stood in a ring of women, forming a large circle around the center of the Hall. The men stood outside them, also in a ring, their faces bright with smiles as they stamped their feet and prepared to begin. In the corners, children laughed and giggled as they made their own small circles in imitation of their elders.

Picking up his fiddle, Arnson Pimball sounded the rush of light notes that signaled the start of the dance. When Kaylie Featherfew joined in with her flute, the women bent their knees and began a slow walk to the right, their hands clapping a beat. The men moved in the opposite direction, circling widdershins while their heavy boots made sounds like drums.

Lily watched the faces of the men pass by her as she moved in place between Anne Cooper and old Tressa McSnare. Each one was familiar to her, but she found herself mesmerized as she studied the lines and shadows of eyes and mouths, searching for something that would recall her father's face. As each man passed her, she paused a moment before looking at the next, as though in the time between her father would rise from the dead and come to take his place in the dance, as he had many times before.

When the circles had passed one another and each man had seen each woman's face, the music began to quicken. Kaylie's flute ran like a brook beneath the notes twirling from Arnson Pimball's fiddle, and the dancers prepared to begin the chain in which each woman grasped the hand of the man across from her and the circles intertwined, with each woman spinning around each man and moving on to the next. Stopped across from her childhood friend Peter Layman, Lily reached out and took his hand in hers.

Immediately, she was struck by a vision of Peter as an old man, his children, yet to be born, gathered around him as he lay dead upon his bed. The image was a peaceful one, and Lily sensed nothing but love in it, but its impact was as if someone had struck her in the head with a rock. It overwhelmed everything else, and she could feel every emotion as though it were her own. She knew the confusion felt by Peter's youngest daughter as she looked into her father's face. She sensed the separation that was just beginning to soak into the heart of his widow as she gazed into the future and saw herself alone. All of these things exploded into her mind in a single instant, battering her with sensations.

Before she had time to recover, she was passed to the next waiting hand, belonging to Hugh Van Woojin, whose cows provided the village with milk and cheese. As his calloused fingers closed around hers, the vision of Peter's death was swept from her head and replaced with one of Hugh, his face contorted in agony, stretched in the field while his cows looked down at him with puzzled expressions on their placid brown faces. Lily felt the crazy jump of Hugh's heart as it beat out of time and pain shot through his chest. She saw clearly the heavy stone he had just attempted to lift, and felt the rawness of his skin where it had fallen from his hands as he'd stumbled under its weight. Then his eyes opened, taking in the familiar faces of his herd and the sun flashing above them, and he died.

Again Lily felt herself passed to another hand, and again a vision came. A vision of death. She closed her eyes tightly and tried to concentrate on the music. She attempted to grasp onto the notes that tumbled from Arnson Pimball's fingers and ride them, letting them lift her above the pictures that flashed across the wall of her skull like the ever-shifting images of a kaleidoscope. But time and again she was jolted away from the music as first one scene and then another played itself out in the moments during which she touched the hands of the people she'd known all her life. She saw how each would die, most peacefully, but some in great pain.

The dance became faster, and Lily felt as though she were being twirled in seven directions at once as her body spun and swayed, kept afloat by hands that, while holding her up, were also the cause of constant terror. Her blood shrieked in her veins, and she felt her skin grow overheated until she was sure she would burst into flame. Through the haze of her visions, she saw their faces, laughing and gay, dodging in and out of sight. What must she look like to them? Did a bright smile cover the dizzying fall she was taking inside of herself? She wanted to scream for them to stop, but as when she saw her father's death, her throat was locked. All she could do was surrender herself to the movement around her and hope that it would end before she was torn apart.

Tableau after tableau bloomed and died in her mind while the music played on. She saw Gudrun Caster felled by a sliver of lightning, and Arles Hewer taken by the vengeful shade of his brother, Shane Egan choking on the bone of a haddock and Molly Pillsin leaping from the cliffs afterwards with their child still in her belly. She saw women and men in their beds, dead while sleeping, their eyes closed as if in dreams. She saw hanged men and women killed by poisons. She saw a woman trampled by a horse and a man whisked into the darkness as the Fair Folk lifted him out of his boat. Most painful for her were the drownings, the faces floating up blue and lifeless as her father's had. One after the other they came, and she was helpless against them.

Then the music stopped, and Lily fell to the floor. As quickly as they'd come, the visions swept out of her mind, leaving her shivering and empty. She opened her eyes, and saw that people were staring down at her, concern worrying their faces. Maxon Ashe reached down to help her up, and she twisted away. "No!" she yelled in a hoarse voice. "Don't touch me!"

Maxon drew back, confused. Lily couldn't tell him that only moments ago she'd seen him mauled by a bear hungry from a long winter of starvation. She only knew that if he touched her the vision would return, and that her heart would tear from any further pain. She lay on the floor and wept while around her people spoke in whispers of madness and enchantment.

Then Alex Henry's face broke through the crowd, and he was beside her as he'd been that morning. "The visions," she said softly. "They've come back."

• FOUR •

BABA YAGA LEANED over the side of the mortar and looked down at the tops of the trees as she passed over them. It was night, and the moon was full, silvering everything beneath it so that the forest appeared to be a sea. The smell of fir and pine floated on the warm summer air, and owls flew alongside her, hooting curiously. All things considered, it was a lovely evening for traveling.

She had not been out of the forest in quite some time. Years, surely. A century or more, possibly. She couldn't really remember. And why had she last left? She thought perhaps it had been to chase down that willful girl, Vasilisa. The one who had stolen her magic skull. She bristled at the memory. How the storytellers had gotten that one so wrong, she would never understand. But it was typical of them. They always cast the young and beautiful as the heroines.

Well, it hardly mattered. The girl was long dead and turned to dirt, while she was alive and flying through the summer night on an adventure. Still, she wished she had the skull back. It was a useful thing to have. She made a note to go in search of it when she returned, then promptly forgot all about it again.

She looked up at the stars. Above her, the Swan was being chased through the sky by the Fox. In a few hours the Crippled Child would make his way through the darkness, dragging the dawn behind him. She yawned and closed her eyes. She slept very little now, often going years without stretching out in her big feather bed. But the gentle rocking of the mortar made her tired, and so she made a nest of straw and feathers in the bottom of her vessel and lay down, curling into a ball so that her knees were tucked against her chin.

It was not long after that the mortar passed over Lily's village. Baba Yaga opened one eye. She kept very still, listening to the music. When it abruptly stopped, she commanded the mortar to descend. It landed just outside the doors of the Great Hall, and Baba Yaga climbed over the side and went to the nearest window. She pressed her face against it and peered inside.

The girl was lying on the floor, surrounded by her people. For a moment Baba Yaga thought she might be dead, and was surprised to find that this disappointed her. Then a man reached out to help the girl and the girl came to life, crying out as if she were afraid. Baba Yaga nodded. *You should be afraid,* she thought. *This is just the beginning.*

She watched for another minute or two, then turned and hobbled back to the mortar. As it rose into the sky, she heard the music begin again. Then she passed over the houses and flew out towards the sea. In the cemetery on the point, a brokenhearted bride's ghost paused at the edge of the cliff and for the first time in three hundred years looked up in wonder before stepping off and falling to the rocks below.

• FIVE •

By the afternoon of the next day, everyone in the village knew of Lily's curse. While certainly accustomed to the workings of magic, few had seen it manifested in such a powerful way, and the result was that Lily was looked upon with a mixture of fear and awe. Those who could remember the last time such a thing had happened passed glances between themselves and remained silent, knowing as they did that speaking of such things could cause the forces that brought them into being to behave in strange and unpredictable ways. Instead they made garlands of bird bones and dried violets and hung them on their doors.

Lily herself remained in her room, staring out at the sea and trying not to look at her hands. From time to time she picked up the mirror her father had given her and gazed at her reflection. Again she saw the bones of another girl floating beneath the smooth surface of her cheeks and the curve of her lips, and she hated what she saw. She closed her eyes, willing the girl who carried such terrible power in her hands to die, leaving behind the one who knew nothing of death. But each time she opened her eyes and saw that the other girl was still there, growing stronger with each passing day.

Through it all, her mother remained in her bedroom. She, too, had heard talk of Lily's gift. Only unlike the villagers, she was certain that she knew well its origins, and she had spent her time on her knees in prayer to a god the villagers had no use for, and in fact had never heard talk of. It was the god of her own childhood, and she found herself crying out to him to remove from Lily whatever evil had crept into her soul and corrupted her in such a hideous way as to make her every touch open up a portal to death.

Lily could hear mumbled words floating stillborn through the house. She had no idea what her mother was doing, and was thankful only that she remained in her room and left Lily to clothe herself in a new body. She knew that her father's death had changed something between herself and her mother, that her mother blamed her for what had happened. She knew her mother feared her in the same way she herself feared the girl moving about inside her skin, but she understood also that she would get no help in her fight.

And then her mother opened the door and announced that they were leaving the village that evening. She told Lily to pack one bag and to be ready to go when dusk descended and made it possible to pass out of the village.

Lily had never left the village. Few had. And only one—her father—had ever returned. He had refused ever to speak about what he'd seen, and likewise demanded that his wife never talk of her life before coming to her new home. This she had done out of love for him, although over time it had made her bitter and afraid, and in the end she had hated him almost as much as she loved him. The village she had always feared, and now that her husband was dead and her daughter possessed of evil, she longed for escape.

Like most of the people who lived there, Lily had given little thought to what lay beyond the lands she knew. Now, faced with the thought of leaving, she found herself very afraid. She feared also the urgency she heard in her mother's voice, and the way in which her eyes stared past Lily as though looking at something looming dark and dangerous behind her.

Still, she knew that leaving was what she had to do, not for her mother's sake, but for her own. She needed to run from the village and from the sea, away from the pull of its tides that drowned men and called women to throw themselves into the waves. She knew it was the tides that had summoned the blood from between her legs and woken the other girl, who fought even now to claw her way through muscle and bone to lay waste to Lily's world. Lily could feel her fingers working their way through knots of blood in search of the door that would free her forever. Perhaps, she thought, running away from the sea would make the girl drowsy and lull her into a false sleep.

She packed quickly, filling a small bag with clothes. She put into it the hand mirror and the box with the shell, and then she was ready. She went downstairs and found her mother waiting. She too had packed almost nothing, choosing to leave behind that which belonged in the place she had been taken to by her husband. She had on the dress she had worn on the evening she'd arrived in the village, and a small hat perched on her head. Everything else remained in the house, which she left quickly and without looking back.

Once or twice as they walked down the lone road away from the village Lily saw her mother look back, as though expecting someone to be following them. But Lily knew that no one would try and stop them. People came and left the village by choice, not by force, and it was understood that no one who left ever spoke of its existence to anyone else. Even if they should, it would be impossible for someone not born into the village to find his way there.

After half an hour, they came to the bridge that passed over the river that marked the village's easternmost edge. Surrounded as it was on the west, north, and south by the sea, the bridge provided the only way in or out of the village, not that many ever crossed its wide wooden boards. Sometimes the children, filled with the flighty courage common to the very young, would dare one another to step foot on it, but none ever got more than a few feet onto its expanse before turning and running back to the safety of the rocks that sat at the entrance, where they stood with hearts beating, laughing at their own fear as they looked into the thick fog that perpetually covered the far side of the bridge, even on the finest summer day.

As Lily and her mother approached the bridge, Lily's heart began to sing wildly in her chest. With darkness nipping at their heels, she knew that they must cross over quickly or risk doing business with whatever dark creatures wandered the borders at night. The fog swirled before her, turning over and over upon itself like a large grey cat rolling in the grass. She looked into its grizzled center and wondered where it would take her.

Her mother started forward uneasily, her footsteps unsure as she tested the bridge, perhaps half afraid it would give way beneath her shoes. But it held, and soon they were approaching the veil of fog. Lily closed her eyes and allowed her mother to pull her into it. She felt the cool wet kiss of air around her as they passed through, and the sound of their feet became duller and somehow sadder.

Then it was over. When Lily opened her eyes again, she was standing on the other side of a bridge beneath a sky dark with night and lit by the thin breath of a moon that seemed smaller than the one that hung over the village. The air was warm, and she could not smell the sea. When she turned around, she saw that the bridge she had just crossed simply made a small jump over a trickling stream before continuing on down a dusty road.

"Where are we?" she asked her mother. "Where is the village?"

Her mother hushed her. "There is no village. There never was. Now follow me."

Her mother began walking down the road under stars, and Lily followed. She had no idea where she was or where they were going, and she wondered about the village. She wondered, too, if in crossing over the bridge she had left behind the girl she was trying to kill. She made her hands into fists, searching them for any signs of her presence, but she felt nothing but the comforting cushion of flesh plump with fat.

They walked in silence for half an hour. Lily listened to the sounds of crickets in the fields on either side of the road and to the wind rustling the leaves over her head. While every now and again she would see the shape of something creep out of the tall weeds and peer at her for a moment before slipping back into the dark, she sensed that she had nothing to fear from anything that lived in the woods whose trees rose up into the sky beyond the seas of grass.

Rounding a turn in the road, Lily saw ahead of them the lights of a town. They shone harshly over the fronts of houses, filling the air with a hard white glow that hurt Lily's eyes and made her blink. As they left the fields and woods behind and made for the streets lined with cars, she felt a strong desire to turn and run. Yet the hum of the electrical lines over her head drew her deeper in with their voices, and she found herself anxious to see what lay beyond the quiet doors.

Her mother walked down the main street as though she'd been reborn. Her gaze leapt from building to building. "It's still the same," she said, her voice that of a little girl seeing her first circus. "It's just as I remember it the night we passed through."

"Passed through?" Lily asked. "You mean when you came to the village with father?"

Her mother turned to her, her eyes dark. "I told you not to speak of the village," she said. "If anyone asks you, we're from Pilotsville."

Lily nodded, afraid to say anything that might make her mother angry. She didn't understand why the village should remain a secret any more than she understood why they were in the town, but she knew that it was important to not draw any more attention to herself than was necessary. The girl within her fed on attention, and if she was still there, waiting, Lily was determined to starve her into death.

Her mother led her to the door of a building where a bright blue sign blinked like a startled child. GOOD EATS it said, bursting into indigo life and then dying again a moment later, only to be resurrected as Lily held her breath waiting to see if each time would be the last, marveling when it was not. She peered in the windows and saw a room filled with tables. People sat at them, laughing and talking, and a woman wearing a red and white checked apron brought them plates of food.

Lily's mother pushed open the door and led Lily inside. To her surprise, no one looked up to stare at them. The woman in the apron merely waved at them to take a table in a far corner. Lily sat down on the red bench and winced at the feel of the odd material, hot and sticky against her bare legs. She slid into the corner of the booth, where she could see everything in the room. She kicked her feet against the floor as she looked around.

The people at the other tables looked much like the people in the village, but somehow less colorful, as though time had faded them in the way that repeated washings pulled the dye from cloth. Their faces showed the strain of wear, and they seemed tired despite their laughter. Still, their clothes were the clothes of working people, and that made Lily feel more at ease.

The woman in the apron approached the table and handed Lily and her mother each a piece of paper. "What can I get you to drink?" she asked.

Lily looked at her mother, unsure of what to say. "Water," her mother said, "and two orange sodas."

The woman left, and Lily looked at the piece of paper she'd been handed. Written all over it were the names of different kinds of foods, some of which she recognized and many of which she didn't. "What is this?" she asked her mother.

"It's a menu. This is a restaurant, where people eat. Pick something from the menu and order it."

Lily had never heard of such a thing, but the idea of being able to eat what she liked appealed to her. She ran her eyes up and down the lists of foods, trying to decide what to have. When the waitress returned with their drinks, she was ready.

"I'd like a hamburger," she said. She wasn't sure what it was, but she liked the name of it.

"Do you want cheese on that?" the waitress asked.

Lily nodded.

"How about fries?"

Again she nodded, although she couldn't imagine what the woman would bring her. She was thankful when the woman turned her attention to her mother.

"I'll have a tuna sandwich," her mother said. "With lettuce."

The woman retreated, and Lily picked up the glass that had been set in front of her. It was filled with orange soda, and the tiny bubbles that ran up the side of the glass fascinated her. She brought the glass to her lips and sipped. Her throat filled with the tart taste of orange, followed almost immediately by a sickening sweetness and a rush of fizzy air that tickled her nose and made her choke. She quickly put the glass down and took a swallow of water. Again she choked, this time because the water tasted dead to her.

"That's awful," she said, thankful at least to have the horrible sweet taste out of her mouth.

"Things are different here," her mother said. "You'll get used to it. You'll have to."

Lily decided that the time was right for asking questions. "Where are we going?"

Her mother's mouth was set in a firm line. "I don't know yet."

"Is this where you came from?" Lily said. "Before—"

"No. I lived in a big city. Now don't ask anything else. Just remember that if anyone asks, we're from Pilotsville, and we're on our way to visit a friend."

The waitress returned carrying two plates. She set them on the table. "Enjoy." She smiled. Lily smiled back. Something about the simple way in which the woman moved through the room calmed her.

She picked up the hamburger and took a big bite. She expected it to make her gag, as the drink had, but she was surprised to find that she enjoyed the taste. She gobbled, amazed to find that she was much hungrier than she thought. She picked up a fry and bit into it. Discovering that it was just a length of potato, she delighted in eating the pile on her plate. She couldn't imagine why anyone would want to take ordinary food and do such outlandish things to it, but she enjoyed it nonetheless. Besides, she could feel the food adding to the stores of fat that suffocated the girl inside her.

As she ate, Lily tried to listen to the conversations of people around her. The air was thick with voices, and it was hard to distinguish one from another, but sometimes she could pull a single thread of words from the tangle and make out what was being said. A few tables away, a man and woman were arguing, although no one looking at them could tell. The man was accusing the woman of being unfaithful to him, and she was denying it. Her voice flowed angry and hot on the air, and Lily could tell that she was lying even as she pleaded innocence and picked at her salad.

Near the door, a group of men spoke — they seemed to be happy, and accompanied their talk with much laughter — their conversation centered on their work at a nearby factory, their wildly stupid boss, and their own unappreciated accomplishments. They appeared to be slightly drunk, and Lily found their behavior comforting in a way she did not entirely understand. Time and again she discovered herself staring at their round, reddened faces and laughing along with them.

Besides the men, the people she found herself watching most intently were a family seated across the room. A mother, father, and daughter sat eating quietly. The girl was about Lily's age, and several times she looked at Lily and smiled, as though their similarity in years made them friends. In contrast to the rest of the diners, the family said very little. Despite their silence, Lily could tell by the way they passed things to one another that they loved each other very much. When the father took his napkin and wiped something from his daughter's face, Lily felt tears begin to flow down her cheeks.

"Stop that," her mother said. "People will stare."

Lily mopped at her face with her own napkin. "I miss him," she said. "Don't you?"

Her mother looked down. "He's gone," she said simply.

Even though she knew and feared the answer, Lily asked the question that she had been thinking since the afternoon of her father's death. "You think I killed him, don't you?"

Her mother remained silent. Lily looked at the half-eaten sandwich on her plate, a row of jagged bread where her teeth had bitten into it. She wanted to snatch it up and hurl it against the wall, to startle her mother out of her silence. She wanted to tell her about the other girl, the girl who had really killed her father, using Lily's hands to do it. She wanted to tell her about how the girl had reached out to the villagers during the dance and fed on their deaths. She wanted her mother to open her arms and take her into them.

But she also knew that it did not matter. The girl inside her slept, coaxed into a drowsy slumber by the lullaby of blood singing in Lily's veins as it beat beneath the layers of fat she had carefully wrought. Even now she felt the warmth of her meal spreading out like a blanket over the sleeping demon, pushing her deeper into hibernation. She picked at the few remaining scraps of food on her plate, thankful for every piece that added to her inner armor.

The waitress arrived again to take away the plates and glasses. As she reached over the table to gather up Lily's mother's unfinished sandwich, she placed a hand on Lily's shoulder. "Can I get you some dessert, honey? We have some nice chocolate cake."

Lily couldn't answer, for the moment the woman's hand touched her, the sleeping girl within her awoke. Lily saw clearly the waitress bent across the counter near the door, a ragged hole gaping in her chest where a gunshot had tattered her skin and blown her heart into scarlet ribbons across the wall behind her. Her mouth was open in surprise, and she still clutched the pencil she carried in her left hand. Stray pieces of paper, bills from the cash register, whirled about her feet.

The woman's hand continued to rest on Lily's shoulder as she waited for a response. As long as it was there, the scene remained fixed in Lily's mind, as though her touch formed a conductor between her soul and Lily's sight like a lightning rod channeled the power of a storm into the ground. She was unable to breathe, yet she could think of no way to remove the woman's hand from her body and break the connection. She looked up into the smiling face while the image of violent death floated over her still-living features like a mask.

"No," Lily was able to whisper. "No, thank you."

"Okay," the woman said cheerfully as the hole in her chest oozed blood onto the white expanse of the counter. "But it's not every day I make my chocolate cake. I'll just bring you the check."

As soon as she removed her hand, Lily felt cool air fill her lungs again. She looked up and saw that her mother was staring at her.

"It happened again, didn't it?" she said stonily.

Lily could only nod. She felt ashamed that she had not been able to keep the creature inside her at bay. She had not done enough.

"I thought maybe it was just that place," her mother said, as though speaking to herself. "I thought getting away would put an end to it."

"I'm sorry," Lily whispered. "I'm sorry."

Her mother said nothing more as she took the check when it came and paid with money that had remained in her purse untouched for more than thirteen years. The bills unfolded like leaves, and the coins clinked as her mother dropped them onto the table. Lily wanted to ask what they were, and what their importance was, but she didn't dare open her mouth.

Her mother stood and put her hat on. She started to reach for Lily's hand, as if to pull her up, and then drew back. "Come on," she said.

Lily followed her out of the restaurant, taking one last glance at the family she had watched throughout her meal. The waitress was putting down two slices of rich dark cake on white plates before the daughter and the mother. One of the slices held a burning candle. As Lily watched, the daughter blew out the candle and took a bite of the cake. Then she pushed the plate towards her father. For a moment their hands touched, and Lily saw that the girl continued to beam with happiness. As Lily and her mother walked out of the restaurant into the shrill electric light, Lily heard the father's voice rise above the others.

"Happy birthday," he said as the door shut with a bang.

• SIX •

NEED ONE RADIO sandwich with grass, then burn one and take it through the garden. And table six wants two cackleberries on a raft and a bowl of graveyard stew for the half-pint."

The waitress slapped the order down and turned away with a weary glance at the new cook. Baba Yaga slipped several pieces of bread into the toaster, then took two eggs from the bowl on the counter and cracked them onto the grill. Checking to make sure the dishwasher wasn't watching, she removed a third egg and popped it into her mouth. The shell crunched, and she sucked the warm yolk between her teeth.

Coming into the restaurant had been an unexpected decision, but it had proved to be a good one. From her vantage point at the stove she could look out at the diners, making it easy for her to observe the girl and her mother. As Baba Yaga fried hash and grilled hamburgers, the two of them sat across from one another, mostly in silence.

It was the mother who interested her most at the moment. She was a peculiar creature, dark-eyed and pretty in a brittle way, like an old painting that had hung too long on a wall touched by the sun. Her beauty was faded but still very much in evidence. Baba Yaga wondered if her years in the village had done this to her, or if it was the natural progression of time alone. Most people, she thought, would have grown younger in the presence of the strong magic that ran beneath the village. The woman must have fought hard against it.

Baba Yaga had learned what she needed to of the woman and her coming to the village from the owls. The birds recalled her arrival as if it had happened only the day before. She had come there hopeful but afraid, they said, and her fear had deepened with each passing year. It was rumored that she prayed to a dead god, and that she quarreled with her husband about dedicating the child to his service. She refused to leave milk for the kobold of the house, or to greet the white squirrels of the wood when she chanced to see them.

This explained a great deal, Baba Yaga thought. The woman and the village were not a good match. Probably the woman and the man had been equally unsuited to one another. These things happened sometimes. But now the man was dead and it no longer mattered. Well, except for the girl. It was the child who would suffer the most because of the mother's unhappiness, of course. That was unavoidable.

"If only she'd been kind to the kobold," Baba Yaga muttered as she opened a can of tuna fish and emptied it into a bowl. "Things might have ended differently."

She added a hamburger to the grill. She knew it was for the girl, and so she watched it carefully so as not to overcook it. In the meantime, she finished the mother's sandwich. The lettuce leaf she placed on the bread was just slightly wilted, perhaps a little brown around the edges. She was mean with the mayonnaise. After adding too much celery to it, she leaned over and spit into the bowl before spreading the mixture over the bread.

When the hamburger was done, she plated it prettily, topping it with slices of tomato and onion, then adding a mound of crisp fried potatoes fresh from the oil and sprinkled with just the right amount of salt. Then she tapped the little silver bell that summoned the waitress. She watched as the plates were delivered to the table, waiting until she saw the expression of discovery on the girl's face after she took her first bite. Satisfied, she removed her apron and handed it to the surprised dishwasher.

"I quit," she said, and walked out the door.

• SEVEN •

Outside, the echo of the man's words mingled with the scattered sounds of passing cars, barking dogs, and the tired, happy laughter of children playing games in the late summer darkness. All wove together in a chorus that filled Lily's head and made her very disoriented. She felt out of place and out of time, as though a great force had ripped her away from everything she knew and deposited her, dizzy and breathless, on a strange mountaintop. Even her mother was unfamiliar to her. For the first time in her life, she felt completely alone.

Her mother walked briskly down the sidewalk. Lily had no choice but to follow her, but she remembered how her mother had looked at her in the restaurant, and she didn't dare ask where they were going. Instead, she looked about her, taking in the town as they passed through it. Moving away from the excited shine of electric lights, the town became less busy. The shadows cast by clouds rolling over the moon wrapped everything in soft blankets, making them appear like giant puppets and animals, and Lily wondered what it would all look like in the daylight. The houses sat quiet as stones, and in some the windows burned brightly. From time to time a child would appear from behind a tree, darting through a yard while another child followed in chase, reaching out to grab a flapping shirt tail or braid. Then they would be gone, and all Lily would hear was the sound of their voices like the calls of nightbirds.

They walked all through the town, past houses and churches (although Lily didn't know what those were and wondered at the pointed roofs topped by crosses) and the school, past a hardware store and a library and even a small movie theater, where groups of girls and boys Lily's age stood in loud brassy knots and, a few, in nervous pairs. As she passed them, Lily looked into their faces and wondered how many of them were fighting unwanted visitors within their bodies at the same time as they chewed gum and told one another great lies about their lives and who they really were.

Passing another block of houses, they came to a gas station where a lone attendant rested in a chair, leaning up against the peeling wall of the building. A line of brightly-colored flags strung from the garage to a light pole flapped sadly in the warm night air, and a jumble of moths flapped around the lone bulb that spat dirty yellow light over the man as he sat with crossed arms, waiting for cars to come through. There were streaks of shiny black grease across his unshaven cheeks, and his stained shirt had the name BURNELL stitched across the pocket in white thread.

When Lily and her mother approached, the man opened his eyes, pushed back his cap, and smiled a crooked smile. His gaze wandered up and down Lily's mother's body, then moved on to Lily. The way in which he looked at her made Lily feel that he was seeing past her face to that of the girl inside. She could feel the girl's heart begin to beat more strongly beneath her own, and she knew that the man's attention was making her restless. She shifted her eyes from the man's face to the dirt beneath his chair, which was covered with the discarded remains of the cigarettes he smoked one after the next.

As if reading Lily's thoughts, the man pulled a cigarette from the crumpled pack in his pocket and lit it with a match he sparked to life with his fingernail. He drew in and then blew out a cloud of smoke, which drifted down over his face as he spoke. "What can I do for you ladies?"

Lily's mother cleared her throat. "Can you tell me where the bus stops? The bus to Pilotsville? I think it comes through here. At least it did the last time I was here."

The man nodded. "Still does," he said. "Matter of fact, it should be through in about ten minutes."

Lily glanced up and saw that the man was staring at her again. She stared back, searching his eyes for a moment, then looked up at the moths courting the light bulb and let the light fill her head until she saw spots and forgot what had been in his eyes.

"Well, I guess we'll just wait then," her mother said. "I guess we'll just wait right over here. Thank you."

Her mother went and stood on the sidewalk, her shoes as close to the edge as she could get without being in the street. She held her purse tightly and peered intently down the street, waiting for the faint glimmer of headlights. Lily stood behind her, feeling the man's eyes on her skin and sensing each time another eddy of smoke flowed from his dirty lips and crept along the ground towards her. The backs of her legs ached from standing so stiffly, and all she wanted to do was find someplace to sit down.

Right on schedule, the bus came crawling down the street. It pulled up in front of the gas station with a hiss like a hundred horses sighing, and the doors opened. Lily's mother started up the stairs, and Lily stepped on behind her.

"Two tickets to Pilotsville," her mother told the driver, a young man with closely-cropped hair and large teeth.

The man grinned, making his teeth seem even bigger. "Sorry," he said. "This bus only goes as far as Salvation. Special charter for the big meeting there. Wouldn't even be stopping here except as I need gas."

"When's the next bus to Pilotsville?" her mother asked.

"Tomorrow morning," the driver said. "All the buses tonight are only going to Salvation."

Lily's mother sighed. "Well, I guess it's better than nowhere. Maybe we can find someone there to take us to Pilotsville."

"Never know what you'll find in Salvation," the young man said, handing her two tickets and taking the money she took from her bag.

Lily and her mother started down the aisle of the bus as the man shut the doors and pulled away. The seats were filled with people talking to one another, eating sandwiches, and knitting. Many of the people were reading black books, their lips moving silently as they turned the thin pages. Towards the back of the bus there were two empty seats, one on either side of the aisle. Lily's mother sat in one, and Lily slipped into the other beside an old woman whose white hair looked as soft as lamb's wool. She was clutching one of the black books in her tiny hands, and there was a bouquet of sunflowers on her lap.

The woman smiled at her, and Lily smiled back. She was thankful to be sitting. It was very hot, but the motion of the bus as it rolled along created a small breeze that darted in the open window and played with her hair. She shut her eyes and let the steady rhythm of the wheels settle into her bones. She had never been on a bus before, or even in a car, and she felt as though she'd been swallowed up by a large animal that was now running down a road as she floated in its belly.

Outside the bus, the night sped along beside her as the town was left behind and a flat stretch of road rolled ahead of them, disappearing into the blackness. Lily was tired, and she almost wished the bus would roll on forever while she slept. She didn't know where she would be when the doors opened again, but she knew that, wherever it was, she would still be unhappy and she would still be carrying the girl who brought death inside of her.

Just as she was beginning to drift off to sleep, Lily heard someone begin to sing. The voice came from behind her, rising up like a crow and flapping around in the air. "Jesus is my King," said the voice in an ancient warble. "Jesus is my Lord."

Another voice took up the song, and soon the bus was filled with the sounds of many different voices mingling in happy, if not exactly tuneful, joy. "Jesus is my King. Jesus is my Lord. I'm coming home to see Him with gladness in my heart."

Raised from sleepiness by the singing, Lily sat up and looked around. All throughout the bus, men, women, and children were joining in the song. Some began to clap, and soon the bus was vibrating with the sounds of hands slapping together. Lily looked over at her mother, who had fallen asleep and somehow managed to stay so despite the rousing activity. Her head tilted to one side, and her lips were parted slightly.

"How come you all aren't singing?" asked the woman next to her in a gentle voice.

"I don't know the words," Lily said.

The old woman smiled. "It's one of my favorites," she said. "We always sing it at the meetings. You'll learn it there. You are going to the meeting, aren't you?"

"I don't know about the meeting," said Lily. "We're just on our way to Pilotsville."

"You should come to meeting," the woman said. "Nothing like it at all anywhere in the world."

Lily was filled with curiosity. "What kind of meeting is it?" she asked.

"Why, the Reverend Silas Everyman's Holy Gospel Caravan, of course," said the woman. "Don't you know it?"

"We're not from around here," said Lily.

The woman laughed. "Reverend Silas's known everywhere. He's a miracle worker. The Lord touched him when he was a child, and ever since then he's been doing His work."

"What kind of work?" asked Lily.

"Healing," the woman said. "Saving souls, fighting the Devil himself. He has the power of Jesus, he does. Last year at meeting he put his hands on Bessie Crauck and took the cancer right out of her. I saw it myself. And, oh, his preaching. You should see the souls rush to his feet when he gives the call."

Lily was confused. "He puts his hands on people?" she asked.

The woman nodded. She held up her own small, delicate hands and pressed them out towards Lily. "He lays them on you," the woman said, her eyes filled with wonder. "And the spirit of the Lord himself moves through him and into you. Bessie said it was like receiving an electric shock it was so powerful. Right near lifted her off her feet."

"And this heals people?"

"Burnt Bessie's cancer clean out of her," the woman said. "Praise Jesus."

Lily put her hands in her lap and dug the nails into her palms. "Can he do anything else?"

"He can do anything," said the woman. "I've seen him make the blind see and the lame walk. I've seen old men throw out their canes and dance just from his touch. Child, the Reverend Silas Everyman is God's messenger and instrument, plain and simple."

Tears ran down the woman's face as she held her hands up again. "Praise Jesus, he saved me."

Lily couldn't help but stare at the woman as she cried. Nothing of what she said made any sense to Lily, but she seemed to believe that the Reverend Everyman could work magic. And the talk about his hands made Lily wonder if, like herself, he saw what others couldn't. She wondered if he knew how to stop the magic as well, and if he could take it from her hands into his. Her head half-filled with thoughts, she settled back into her seat and listened as the chorus of voices rose up in a great fountain and broke over her head.

After an hour had passed during which the passengers had sung dozens of songs and shouts of "Praise Jesus!" had sailed out the windows like candy wrappers tossed into the wind and left to blow about the lonely highway, the bus pulled off the paved road onto a dirt one. It bumped and ground its way for another twenty minutes until, cresting a hill, it descended into a valley filled with cars and trucks and people.

"It's Salvation!" cried the woman next to Lily, and the passengers cheered.

Lily peered out the window and saw that the bus was headed for what looked like a small village lit with colored lights that twinkled on and off in random patterns. She saw hundreds of people walking excitedly towards the village, their faces alive with smiles. Even the children being dragged or carried along seemed filled with excitement, despite the fact that most of them should have been asleep hours ago.

The bus came to a stop, and the people gathered up their things and filed off quickly. Lily and her mother were the last to leave, stepping out into the sea of scurrying people and pressing against the side of the bus so as not to be swept up in it.

"We have to find a bus that's leaving here," her mother said. "There has to be a way out."

Lily wasn't listening. She felt something in the air, a feeling of excitement that flowed out of the bodies of the people rushing by her and made her head swim. They were all eager to see something, and Lily knew that what they were so eager to see was Reverend Silas Everyman. Again she thought about what the woman on the bus had said, and she made a decision. While her mother scanned the plain of cars for a bus, she stepped quickly into the crowd and was carried away towards the lights.

· EIGHT ·

HE SINGING WAS starting to annoy Baba Yaga.

"Jesus is my King," warbled the woman behind her, very loudly and very much in Baba Yaga's ear.

"King," Baba Yaga said, snorting. "There's nothing so very special about a king. They die like any other man. Usually worse, because somehow they don't think it will ever happen to them. That's the fault of their mothers."

"Jesus is my Lord," the woman shouted.

Baba Yaga turned to the child seated beside her. The girl was perhaps eight or nine years old. She was part of a family of twelve that was scattered throughout the bus. To her credit, she had sat quietly with her hands in her lap for the duration of the ride. Baba Yaga attributed this to the fact that with so many siblings, she was probably used to not being heard, and had simply given up trying.

"Who is this Jesus?" Baba Yaga asked her.

The girl blinked bright blue eyes. "The son of God," she said.

Baba Yaga sighed. "Which one?" she said impatiently.

The girl seemed not to understand the question.

"Which god?" Baba Yaga tried.

The girl shrugged. "Just God. Him." She pointed to the roof of the bus, as if the father of Jesus was perched up there.

"Don't be dim," said Baba Yaga. "It's tiresome."

The girl turned away, not even having the sense to understand that she was very close to being eaten. Baba Yaga considered pinching her, but couldn't muster the enthusiasm for it.

"I'm coming home to see Him with gladness in my heart," exclaimed a chorus of voices.

Baba Yaga began humming to herself, a wild tune she had learned as a girl. She'd long forgotten the words, but the melody remained, haunting the halls of her memory. It was, she thought, something about a man who had lost his true love to a wolf. Or perhaps the man had fallen in love with a wolf. Whatever the case, the tune fought against the singing of the bus passengers.

As she hummed, Baba Yaga sought out the girl called Lily. She sat a few rows up, on the other side of the aisle. She was talking with her seatmate, and seemed interested in whatever conversation they were having. Baba Yaga wished she were sitting closer, or that the people singing would be quiet. Now they were clapping as well, making it utterly impossible to hear anything other than their inane voices.

She closed her eyes and tried to concentrate on her own song, but the man and the wolf slipped away from her. The melody stumbled, then died away as Jesus the King rose up triumphant and filled the world with his glory.

"Jesus is my Lord," sang the girl next to Baba Yaga, her voice thin and wavering.

Baba Yaga glared at her, and the girl stuck out her tongue.

"Maybe there's hope for you after all," Baba Yaga said. She admired this show of defiance from the child, however small it might be and however much it was directed at her. It showed that the girl had some spirit. Probably not enough to ever become someone interesting, but maybe. If the world didn't crush her.

She glanced again at Lily. The girl was looking out the window with a hopeful expression. Something had changed. Baba Yaga wondered what it was. She would find out soon enough, she imagined. In the meantime, she closed her eyes and cursed Jesus the King and the god who sired him.

• NINE •

HE CROWD MOVED around her in swift eddies, people talking in excited voices and pointing towards the colored lights blinking like electric berries. Lily found herself filled with a growing sense of excitement as she lost herself in the shifting patterns of people. The air was warm and filled with a sweet smell, and she quickly forgot about her mother.

After several minutes, she came to the edge of the village, and she saw that it was actually a group of tents arranged in row after row. They were striped in red and white, and from each one flags fluttered like clothes on a line. The lights she had seen were strung between the tents, covering everything in a galaxy of colored stars.

"Come inside," said a woman standing on a small platform that rose up out of the crowd. She had wings like an angel, and her blonde hair fell around her shoulders in waves. She leaned out over the crowd, beckoning to them with a long, delicate finger tipped in gold. "Welcome to the Holy Gospel Caravan," she said, her voice filled with joy. "Come inside and see the miracles of the Lord."

Lily stared up at her, transfixed, while people moved around her to enter the tent city. The woman's wings shimmered gold and blue in the lights, and she seemed to float in the air as she called to the people in her sing-song voice. The woman looked down at her and smiled. "Come," she said, looking into Lily's eyes. "See the miracles awaiting you inside. Come find what you are looking for."

The crowd jostled Lily, and she allowed herself to be pushed along until she was standing among the tents, clutching her small bag of belongings to her chest as she tried to figure out what to do next. As she looked around, she saw that the tents all held different things. On one side of her was a row of booths offering games. Inside them, wheels spun and rows of bottles waited to be knocked down by people throwing balls. On the other side were tents with closed flaps. Standing outside each one was a strangely-dressed person calling out to tell the people what was inside.

Lily walked down the row of tents, looking at each one. She wasn't sure where she was going, and didn't even know really what she was searching for. She wondered where she would find the Reverend Silas Everyman. She knew he must be somewhere inside the tent city, but she had no idea where.

"You there," said a loud voice. Lily looked around. A clown was staring at her. His face was painted white, and there were large red dots on his cheeks. His hair was an explosion of yellow, and he was dressed in a baggy suit of white and blue silk. He danced over to where Lily stood, his feet making big jumps through the air. When he reached her, he held up his hands, which were also white.

"Would you like to see a trick?" he said.

Lily nodded.

The clown grinned and rolled his eyes. He reached behind Lily's ear and pulled out a white flower. He held it out to her, laughing. He leaned towards her, "It's the flower of salvation," he whispered. "Picked just for you."

Lily was puzzled. The flower was beautiful, but she didn't understand what the man was asking her. She remembered how her mother had exchanged coins for food. "I have no money."

The man laughed. "You can't buy the flower," he said. "You must simply ask for it. Do you want it? Do you want salvation?"

Lily looked at the flower in the clown's hand. Then she looked at his face. Close up, she saw that some of the white makeup had worn away in spots, and that beneath it she could see his skin. There was a long scar running the length of his cheek, and the makeup was caked over it in a thick line. His eyes inside their blue circles of paint were bloodshot, and stared at her in much the same way that the man at the gas station had.

She turned and ran away, pushing her way through the crowd and making several turns between the rows of tents. She hoped he wasn't following her, and when she looked behind her, she was relieved to see that he was nowhere to be seen.

She stood in the small space between two tents and listened. Somewhere in the distance she heard the sound of music playing. It was a sad, lonely tune played on a flute, and it reminded her of the sea and twilight and feeling alone. It seemed to rise above the tents and spread out over the tops of the flags.

Listening for the music to tell her where to go, Lily worked her way deeper and deeper into the tent village. She passed tents filled with people singing, animals dressed in coats and hats, and a man walking on legs twelve feet high. She saw a little girl eating a purple cloud from a stick, and three boys riding one bicycle. But none of it interested her enough to abandon the call of the music.

She turned a corner and saw the tent she was looking for. The flap hung partially opened, and the music poured from the inside like a thin stream of clear water. The flag fluttering at the pinnacle of the tent was blue, and there was a crescent moon on it. Unlike the rest of the place, the tent was not surrounded by throngs of curious people looking inside or hanging around waiting to see who went in or out. It was oddly quiet, and Lily was all alone as she approached.

She peered past the flap and saw that the inside of the tent was filled with flickering light from many burning candles, and in the center was a small table. A woman sat on one side of it, facing the opening to the tent and looking at a series of cards laid out before her. She appeared lost in concentration, and did not look up when Lily entered. Behind her, a small child sat on a low stool.

It was the child who played the flute, although he appeared to be no more than three or four years old. The slender reed sang as he ran his tiny fingers up and down its length, his lips blowing a steady stream of air into its throat. When he looked up and saw Lily watching, he stopped playing and looked at her with dark eyes.

I was wrong, Lily thought, unsettled by the way she was being looked at. *It isn't a child at all. It's a very old man.*

The woman seated at the table looked up at Lily. Her eyes shone even in the dim light of the tent, and Lily found herself unable to speak as the woman studied her face.

"The music," she said. "I heard the music and I came."

"What did the song say to you?" asked the woman.

It seemed to Lily an odd question. "It spoke of light and sadness and the heart." She paused. "And it spoke to me of death." She didn't know why she suddenly thought of these things, but she realized that she had been thinking them all along as she followed the music to the tent.

"You heard its words well. Come." The woman gestured to the empty chair across the table from her own.

Lily went to the chair and sat. She looked at the cards on the table. They were covered in pictures, and when she looked at them she felt her mind filling with voices.

"The cards," the woman said. "Do they speak to you as well?"

Lily nodded.

"Then let us see what they can tell us." The woman gathered up the cards into a deck and began to shuffle them. They floated between her hands like feathers as she mixed them up, and they made no noise. Lily watched as she divided the cards into three piles.

"Pick one," the woman said.

Lily reached out a hand and tapped the center pile. The woman took it up and laid nine cards out, face down. One by one, she turned them over, until all but the last was revealed. Lily looked at the pictures: a house, a ship, a snake, a whip, a fish, a mountain, a bear, and a coffin.

Looking at the cards, Lily found that she could see in them something that she understood. It was not words, nor was it music. It was as though each card acted as a mirror reflecting back into her mind a different piece of a picture. The pieces shifted, moving first one way and then another as she tried to put them all together. Occasionally, for just an instant, Lily would get a glimpse of what they were saying. She would feel that she was just about to see something clearly, but before she could fully see it, the pieces would begin moving again.

"I don't understand," Lily said. "What are they saying?"

The woman smiled. "They speak differently to each of us," she said.

"It takes time to understand them. Try again."

Lily concentrated on the images, focusing her mind on what they were saying to her. And when the voices began to separate from the babbling in her head until eight clear, strong notes formed a chorus, she listened.

"Do you understand them now?" the woman asked.

Lily nodded. "I understand something of it." She reached out and picked up the card with a picture of a house. "This is home," she said, dropping the card and picking up the one showing a ship. "But now I'm on my way to somewhere else."

She picked up the snake card. "She lies," said Lily, not certain of whom she spoke. "Her voice is sweet, but behind it there is pain." She heard the voice of the girl who slept in her belly, and she put the card down before the singing could draw her out.

One at a time, she picked up the remaining cards, telling the woman what she saw in them. Some spoke more strongly to her than others, and some she didn't understand at all. But she looked at each in turn and spoke the words that came to her. "Money. Obstacles. Death."

"Now the last card," the woman said when Lily had looked at all the others. "Turn it over."

Lily picked up the card and looked at it. It showed a cross. As she looked at it, Lily felt her mind fill with a discordant laugh that seemed to come at her from all directions at once, drowning out the other voices until all she heard was its mocking sound. She dropped the card, and her mind emptied.

"What does it mean?" she asked the woman. She felt afraid, and didn't understand why.

The woman didn't respond. She gathered up the cards and placed them with the rest. "You have a gift," she said to Lily. "I can see that. But it is a dangerous one. You are the moon, showing others what is hidden from them. They will come to you for answers, but they will fear you because what you say is true."

"Is that the magic?" Lily asked.

The woman looked up. "Magic?"

Lily told her of Alex Henry, and of her dream. When she was finished, the woman looked sad. "Magic is nearly dead in this place," she said. "The world is old now, and weary. Its people do not see any longer the doorways and windows through which magic moves."

"How do you see?" Lily asked. "Are you not of this world?"

The woman laughed. "Yes, I am of it," she said. "There are still some of us who see, some of us who listen to the old voices."

"What are you doing in this place?" asked Lily.

"Sometimes one comes," she said. "Someone like you. Someone who sees. Someone who is searching."

"What do they find here?" asked Lily. "Magic?"

The woman smiled. "Some think so. And perhaps they are right."

Before Lily could ask another question, the sounds of music burst into the tent. Unlike the song that had brought Lily to the tent, this one was loud and brash, filled with drumbeats, trumpets, and whistles.

"It is time for you to go now," the woman said. "You must go to the music. That is the next step on your road."

"Where will it take me?" Lily asked.

"Go now," the woman said.

"May I come back?" Lily asked.

"If you need me, you will find me," the woman said.

Lily left the tent and began once more to follow the music wherever it would lead her. This time, she had little trouble finding it, as nearly everyone she saw was moving quickly in its direction. She simply moved along with the crowd as it wound its way through the tents, until she came to a large tent that towered over the others. People streamed into it from all sides.

Lily entered the tent. Inside, rows of bleachers lined three sides.

They were crowded with people, all of whom were looking expectantly to the large ring in the center of the tent. A wooden platform had been built in the middle of the ring, and it was decorated with gold stars.

Lily climbed up into the bleachers and sat in the very last row. She had a perfect view of the ring and the stage. All around her, people talked in expectant voices. "When do you think he will come" asked a man wearing overalls and a faded green shirt. "Who will he choose?" said a woman holding a baby on her lap.

"Excuse me," Lily said to the man in the overalls. "Who are we waiting for?"

The man looked at Lily strangely. "Why, the Reverend, of course," he said. He turned back to his companions, all of whom turned to stare at Lily.

She had almost forgotten about the Reverend. Now she recalled what the woman on the bus had said about his healing powers, and she became excited again. All thoughts of the woman in the tent and her cards fled from her mind as she remembered that the woman had said the Reverend could heal people with his hands.

Lily watched as the bleachers filled up with people, until there wasn't a bare spot left to be found. Some people even sat on the floor in the dirt. The lower seats were filled with elderly people, people carrying canes, and fathers and mothers holding children. Lily saw a group of women from the bus sitting across the tent from her. They were holding bouquets of white flowers, and Lily wondered if they'd gotten them from the strange clown she'd met earlier.

The music stopped and the lights went out. The crowd began to shriek and clap. All around her voices cried out. "Praise the Lord," screamed one. "Hallelujah," called another.

The tent remained dark as the crowd worked itself up into a frenzy. People stamped their feet against the wood so that it was as if the tent had a heart and it was beating fiercely. People screamed, cried, and cheered. Lily covered her ears to drown out the sound, but still she felt it rattling through her body.

A light appeared at the top of the tent. The crowd went wild, coming to its feet as the light descended. The sound of a choir singing soared up through the darkness from speakers hung all around the great tent, and the noise was deafening. Lily watched as the light grew closer and closer. She squinted her eyes against the brightness, and was able to make out the shape of someone being lowered to the ground on a small platform.

When the platform was only a few feet above the heads of the people in the top rows of the bleachers, golden lights burst into flower around the stage. A warm glow exploded upwards, and the descending platform was engulfed in the light. Lily saw that a man stood there, his arms stretched out wide. When the crowd saw him, they screamed madly.

"It's him," yelled the woman with the baby, collapsing into her husband's arms.

The platform reached the stage, and the man stepped out. He was dressed all in white. His yellow hair was plastered back against his head and gleamed under the lights that surrounded him. He smiled brightly as he picked up a microphone and waved at the cheering crowd.

"Good evening." He had the warmest, most pleasant sounding voice Lily had ever heard. "And welcome to the Reverend Silas Everyman's Holy Gospel Caravan!"

• TEN •

BABA YAGA WATCHED the fortune teller and the changeling through a hole in the tent. She listened as the woman told Lily's fortune using the cards. Finding it interesting, she decided to see for herself what the future might hold for the girl. And so she sat down in the dirt and took from her pocket a bag made from the skin of a hanged man and tied with the hair of a drowned witch.

She scribed a circle in the dirt with her finger. Then she upended the bag and let its contents fall into the circle: a badger's claw, a lump of gold, the dried heart of an unborn child, a twig from a rowan tree, a scale from a talking salmon, a perfectly-formed mandrake root, a nail, one of her own teeth, the skull of a mouse, a dog's eye, an iron coin from a realm whose name had been forgotten nine centuries ago, an ant trapped in amber, and a living spider.

She sat and looked at the pattern formed by the objects, using the rowan twig to occasionally prevent the spider from wandering out of the circle. What she saw mirrored the story found in the fortune teller's cards. Because of this, Baba Yaga decided that speaking to the woman might be a good idea.

She gathered up the talismans and returned them to the bag, which went back into her pocket. Then she went around to the front of the tent and entered.

"Good evening, Grandmother," the woman said.

"Do you know who I am?" asked Baba Yaga.

The woman nodded. "I do. And I am honored to meet you."

"Yes," said Baba Yaga. "Well." She nodded at the creature standing at the woman's side. "They took your child, then? And left that in its place?"

"My son," the woman said. "When he was three days old."

"They're always doing things like that," Baba Yaga said. "It amuses them. Why didn't you put the changeling on the trash heap and beat it? They might have given you back your own."

"That seemed unkind," the fortune teller replied. "Besides, perhaps each is better off where they are now."

"Hmm." Baba Yaga scratched the expanse of her chin. "And what do you make of the girl? The one who was here earlier."

The woman hesitated.

"I'm not going to eat her, if that's what you're worried about," said Baba Yaga.

"It's not that," said the woman. "I'm just not certain *what* to make of her."

Baba Yaga understood that sentiment. "She's dangerous, that one," she said.

"And also in danger," the fortune teller added.

Baba Yaga shrugged. "Everyone is in danger. Life is dangerous." But she knew the woman was right. She'd seen it for herself in the circle. "It could go either way."

"You're here to watch out for her, then?" the woman asked.

"I don't know why I'm here," Baba Yaga answered. "I just am. I'll figure out the why when the time comes."

"I'll help as I can," said the fortune teller.

Baba Yaga nodded. "That reminds me." Her bones cracked as she sat in the chair at the woman's table. "What can you tell me about this King Jesus?"

• E L E V E N •

AGAIN THE CROWD erupted in a cacophony of clapping hands, stomping feet, and screaming voices. The more they yelled, the bigger the man's smile got. He ran around on the stage, waving his hands in the air to get them to cheer even more loudly, until they were making such a noise that Lily was sure that the bleachers would collapse and the tent would follow soon after, trapping them all beneath its heavy wings.

"Are you happy?" the Reverend bellowed into his microphone. "Are you filled with the spirit of the Lord?"

The people put their hands in the air and yelped with joy, like dogs serenading the moon. They continued until Reverend Everyman lowered his hands, motioning for them to be silent. Instantly, the tent was so quiet that Lily could hear the crickets outside singing to one another. All eyes were fixed on the man on stage, who was standing with his hand over his eyes, as though thinking. Lily held her breath along with everyone else, waiting for him to speak. After what seemed like an eternity, he brought the microphone to his lips.

"Dear Jesus," he said in a hoarse whisper. "I feel your power here tonight in this place."

There were scattered cries of "Amen" and "Yes, Jesus" from the crowd. Lily wondered who this man, this Jesus, was that seemed to have such a hold on the people, but she was even more interested in the Reverend Silas Everyman. She was waiting for him to reveal his powers, and she felt her own palms itching in anticipation.

"Jesus." the Reverend raised his voice. "Come into this place." He paused, as though listening. Then his face broke into a smile that creased his forehead. "I feel Him here," he shouted. "I feel Him here with us! Do you feel Him?"

The people buzzed to life, filling the tent with hallelujahs. Lily felt once more the tingling in her hands, and knew that something was happening. "Amen," she said tentatively, hearing her voice break out into the warm air like an egg spilling its yolk. She looked around, afraid that she had spoken too loudly, but no one looked at her.

"I know you feel it," the Reverend said. "I know the Lord is come upon you good people." He looked up into the stands, pointing a finger in Lily's direction. "He's come upon you," he said, and Lily felt her heart stop in her chest. Then the Reverend turned to the other side of the tent. "And he's come upon you."

Lily's heart jumped back to life, but still she felt the flush left by Reverend Everyman's glance as though she'd been kissed. She clasped her hands together in her lap and felt the power within them.

Reverend Everyman walked to the middle of the stage. A thin spotlight surrounded him as he looked out into the packed tent. "Tonight," he said, "I want to talk to you about sin."

Lily watched as he strode from one side of the stage to the other, looking out at the assembled people, all of whom waited to hear what he would say next. They seemed expectant, as though they knew what was coming and were anxious for it to arrive.

"Sin," said the Reverend, "is all around us. Even now it waits — hidden — until it has an opportunity to reach out and wrap its greedy fingers around our necks. It waits to choke us. It waits to kill us."

He came to the edge of the stage and paused. "Some of you here tonight are struggling with sin." He shook his head, heavy with sadness. "I can feel it, curled up tight in your hearts, eating away at you. I can feel its evil little teeth grinding away, filling you up with its poisonous black breath until you can no longer draw goodness into you."

The Reverend's words filled Lily with fear. He seemed to be describing the ache she felt inside her belly, where the girl who killed her father was kept prisoner. It was as though he saw right inside her and knew what she hid from the world. She listened as he continued, hoping to find some sort of answer to what lay within her.

"Maybe there are some here tonight struggling with the sin of lust," he said. "Who are tempted by thoughts of the flesh. Or perhaps you're struggling with pride." Lily could feel people around her moving uncomfortably, as though the bleachers were too hard.

Everyman held his hands up to the darkness at the top of the tent. "Lord! I feel people in pain. All around me, Lord. The pain of sin. Help them, Lord, to see inside themselves. Help them to recognize the sin and to fight it. With your help, Lord. Through my words, let them hear you."

In the light that remained fixed on him wherever he moved, Lily could see that tears had begun to stain Silas Everyman's cheeks. His voice cracked with emotion as he looked out at the audience.

"I know the pain of sin," he said. "I know how you hurt. And I know how hard it is to wrestle those demons who have a hold on your heart so tight you can feel them squeezing it every minute of your life. But I'm telling you that you must fight them. You must break their hold. For if you don't, you will surely pay the price."

Lily felt herself wanting to reach out to Everyman. While she didn't understand much of what he said, she saw his tears and wanted to wipe them away. More than that, she felt that he knew her, knew what she felt inside and could show her how to fight it so that it never hurt anyone again. She began to understand what the woman on the bus had meant when she talked in awe of the man now on stage speaking. He held the audience in his hand as he spoke to them, and it was impossible not to listen.

"Perhaps there are some of you here tonight," he said "who don't believe what I say, who don't believe in the power of sin. Perhaps there are some of you who don't know what it can do to you."

He turned to the back of the stage and motioned with his hand. The curtains there parted, and out from between them came a tall, thin figure. It was wearing a dress, but a long, thick beard spilled from its chin almost to the floor. The person walked to the front of the stage and stood there, lit all around by a blinding light that caused it to blink repeatedly.

The Reverend came up beside the figure and gestured to it. "This is Martha," he said. "Despite her appearance, she is as human as you or I. In fact, Martha was one of the most beautiful women you've ever seen. She turned heads wherever she went."

He grasped Martha's head in his hands and twisted it towards the light, so that she was forced to look out into the crowd. "Martha has been transformed by sin," Everyman shouted. "She was untrue to her husband, and as a result her beauty was taken from her and replaced by ugliness."

The crowd murmured in horror, staring at the disgraced woman on the stage. "It is too late for Martha," Everyman said. "Sin has ruined her. Just as it will ruin you if you allow it into your life."

Martha turned and walked back to the curtains, disappearing between them. A moment later, they parted again and a man came out. He was dressed in a suit and tie, and appeared to be perfectly normal. Then he stepped into the light, and the crowd gasped, for where his mouth should have been there was nothing but an expanse of smooth skin.

Reverend Everyman gestured to the man's face. "Here you see again the hideous effects of sin," he said. "In Edward's case, the sin of lying. Year after year he told lies — to his friends, to his employer, to his family. He gloried in his ability to bend the truth to suit his purposes. He never listened to the warnings of those who tried to help him, until one day he woke up and saw that the evil he had been speaking had eaten away his tongue and caused his lips to close forever."

Edward looked at his feet as Everyman pointed at him. "A vicious tongue," he said, "is fueled by sin. And look where it leads. How many of you are guilty of harboring Edward's sin inside yourselves?"

Throughout the tent, Lily could see women and men weeping, as though seeing on Edward's face a reflection of their own misery. She felt a sense of horror surrounding her and closing in as she thought of what had befallen the two people she'd just seen. Her mind churned with thoughts of what else might be possible in a world where people were disfigured for their weaknesses.

Everyman ushered Edward to the back of the stage, then faced the crowd again. "And now," he said, "I will show you the saddest sight of all. A child. Nothing but a young girl. A young girl who should be overflowing with innocence." He opened the curtain and led onto the stage a girl. She was small, and she was naked. Her skin seemed to be covered in all manner of strange symbols done in black. Even from her perch high up in the bleachers, Lily thought the girl was the most wonderful thing she had ever seen.

The girl stood on stage, trying to cover herself with her hands while Everyman walked around her. "Look at her," he trumpeted. "See how she is marked by sin. You may be wondering how one so young, so small, could be already stained in such a way." He waited for the crowd to imagine all sorts of terrible pasts for the girl before continuing. "I will tell you how. It's because before her birth her mother gave in to temptation of the worst kind."

The crowd began to buzz, as everyone whispered amongst themselves, trying to figure out what the mother's sin was. Everyman let the expectation build until the tent was humming, then he continued with his story. "I found this girl during my travels over the seas. She cannot speak. She is uncivilized. She was living like a wild animal. When I inquired after her, I was told that her mother was a powerful witch."

At the word "witch," there was more talking in the tent, as people grew more and more excited. Lily found herself shrinking back against the bleachers. She had known some witches in the village, and although all of them had been wise and kind, she knew that there were also witches who practiced a dark magic.

The Reverend held up a hand to silence the crowd. "I was told that the woman had found pleasure with the Devil himself," he continued, bringing even more gasps from the audience. "The child had been born in the manner in which you see her now, forever marked as the product of an unholy union. I found her mother, and demanded of her that she give me the child, that I might save her soul. But she would not listen. She worked magic against me. Said spells. Made charms. She sent demons to torment me in my sleep."

The girl was staring out into the crowd. Despite her shame, Lily sensed in her a defiance, as though she were angry at being displayed before the audience. The girl seemed not to be listening to the words flowing from Everyman's lips. She appeared to be looking out onto a world of her own, one in which no one pointed at her or ridiculed her. It made Lily sad to see her.

"I fought her," he said. "I fought her with prayer and with the power of the Lord, until she fell silent and was no more."

He grabbed the girl by the shoulder and tried to turn her around. When he touched her, she lashed out, kicking him in the shin and spitting. The crowd recoiled in fear. Everyman struggled with the girl, attempting to restrain her by holding her wrists. Still she kicked and cursed him, her feet swinging in arcs that were cut off as she connected with his body.

Two clowns ran onto the stage and grabbed the girl. Shoving her roughly, they pushed her back into the curtains, where she was swallowed up. The Reverend dusted himself off, picked up his fallen microphone, and addressed the stunned crowd.

"As you can see—" He smiled, tight-lipped. "—the child is still under the control of the demons visited upon her soul by her mother. Let this be a lesson to those of you with children that your sin may trickle down into the hearts of your young ones."

Throughout the audience, Lily saw mothers and fathers put arms around their children, pulling them tight. Several of the children had begun to cry after seeing the girl onstage biting and kicking as she was led away, and now their parents attempted to comfort them. Lily thought of her own mother, who had refused to comfort her when she most needed it, and wondered where she was at that moment. She began to scan the audience, looking for a sign of her, but her attention was quickly drawn back to the Reverend Silas Everyman as he leapt off the stage and began walking around the tent.

He made his way to the people sitting in the first few rows. As he neared, people began to reach out their hands to him and to call his name. He stopped and put his hand to his head. "Yes, Lord," he said. "Yes, I hear you. You say to ask for Amy? Is that right, Lord? Amy?"

He looked into the sea of waving hands. "Is there an Amy here?" he asked.

A woman stood up, waving her arms and yelling, "Praise Jesus!" She was very young, but as she pushed her way into the aisle, Lily could see that her left leg was encased in a metal brace. She limped through the dust as she made her way to Reverend Everyman, creating a small cloud of dirt that swirled about her feet when she stopped. She stood before him, wringing her hands and covering her mouth.

The Reverend laid a hand on the woman's shoulder. "Amy," he said. "The Lord tells me that your leg is weak, that it is twisted and you cannot walk." Amy nodded her head, tears flowing freely down her cheeks and falling into the dirt.

"It has been this way since you were a child?"

Amy nodded again. She was saying "Jesus, Jesus, Jesus," over and over as Everyman held her. His eyes were closed, and Lily saw his lips moving silently.

"Do you believe in the power of Jesus, Amy?" the Reverend asked. Amy put her hands in the air and yelled, "Yes, Lord. I believe."

The Reverend put his hand on her forehead. "Lord," he cried out. "Send your power into this believer. And if she truly believes, Lord, then heal her twisted leg."

He gave a slight push, and Amy crumpled to the floor, her useless leg stretched out to one side. Lily watched as several people rushed to her side and began to fan her face. After a minute, Amy opened her eyes and looked around, as though she'd been sleeping and had no idea where she was. Two men helped her to her feet, where she stood swaying slightly.

"Now let her go," the Reverend said.

The two men stepped away, and Lily held her breath, waiting for Amy to fall once more. Instead, she took a tentative step, then another. After she'd walked three steps, she undid the brace and it fell away from her body with a clatter. Then the woman took several more steps.

"She is healed!" Everyman yelled into the microphone. "The power of Jesus Christ the Lord has made her whole!"

The entire crowd rose to its feet to thunderous applause and shouts of "Amen." They all watched as Amy, tears streaming down her face, walked around the perimeter of the tent. When she returned to where Everyman stood, beaming, she fell to her knees, thanking him.

He motioned for her to rise, and the same two clowns who had taken away the girl led her out of the tent. The Reverend moved on to another row of waving people, again closing his eyes and thinking. "Is there a Peter here?" he asked, pointing to a group of people holding up signs that read JESUS IS LORD.

An elderly man stepped forward, helped along by a younger man. "This is my father," said the young man. "His name is Peter."

Everyman stepped up to the pair of men and laid his hand on the older one's head. "Your father is deaf," he said, and the young man nodded.

The Reverend closed his eyes again. "Lord, remove the stoppage from this man's ears. Remove it that he might hear your words, Lord."

The old man staggered back and was caught up in the arms of his son, who righted him again. He looked around, bewildered, and then clasped his hands to his ears as if in pain.

Silas Everyman took the old man's hands in his own and pried them from his head. The man winced. "Can you hear me, Peter?" the Reverend asked. The man nodded his head, looking around in awe as the crowd erupted into bursts of applause.

"Have you ever heard a voice before, Peter?" the Reverend asked.

The old man shook his head. "No," he said in a soft voice. "No." He began to cry, and his son put his arms around his father. "Thank you, Jesus," the younger man cried, hugging his father tightly. "Thank you, Jesus." Then the two escorts came and led them away.

As she watched the Reverend move throughout the tent, laying his hands on one person after another, Lily found herself wishing he would call out her name. She didn't know how he knew which people to pull from the crowd, but each time he spoke, she hoped it would be to call her forth. She wanted to feel his hands upon her head, filling her with whatever power it was that healed the people he touched.

She watched for a long time as Silas Everyman went throughout the crowd, calling out names and healing those who came. She saw blind eyes opened, crippled legs walk, and dying children brought to their feet red-cheeked and healthy. Wherever the Reverend went, healing flowed from his fingers.

After lifting a man in a wheelchair to his feet and sending him on his way, the Reverend returned to the stage. Although many called for him to come back and touch those whom he had not called, he climbed the steps and picked up his microphone. Lily's heart fell as she realized she would not be chosen.

"Thank you, Jesus!" He lifted his hands up over his head. "Thank you for sending your healing power to these people!"

He pointed out over the crowd of standing people. "There are some of you who are still hurting," he said. "Some of you who wonder why your names were not called."

Lily listened carefully to Everyman's words. She sensed he was speaking to her.

"Some of you here tonight do not yet know the Lord Jesus Christ," he said. "And until you do know him, and take him as your savior, you cannot be healed. Like those unfortunate people you saw up on this stage earlier, you are still held captive by sin."

Lily thought about the bearded woman, the man with no mouth, and the naked girl. They all had looked ashamed of what they were. She herself felt ashamed. Ashamed that she had allowed the girl inside her to have her way. Ashamed that she was unable to stop her. Ashamed that she had killed her father.

"Tonight I ask those of you who wish to know the Lord Jesus to come forward. Feel the voice of Jesus calling you to come to him."

Just then, lines of clowns entered the tent. Each was dressed like the one she had seen earlier, the one who had tried to give her a flower. They began to move throughout the crowd, holding out their hands.

"Take the hand of one of my messengers," Everyman was saying. "Take a hand and come to Jesus."

Lily watched as throughout the tent people rose and grasped the offered hands of the men with painted faces. Many were weeping as the clowns led them out of the tent.

"Yes," cried the Reverend. "Answer the call. Stand up and come to the Lord."

One of the white-faced men was climbing the bleachers towards Lily. She watched him move up the rows, holding out his hands to those around him. His painted smile beamed ceaselessly as he worked his way through the people. He was only a few rows in front of her.

"Do you seek the healing power of Jesus?" Everyman shouted. "Do you desire an end to your suffering? Then come."

Lily stood up. Her body seemed to move on its own, and she found herself rising to her feet. Seeing her, the clown turned and reached out his hand. As Lily moved forward to take it, the people around her patted her on the back. "Good girl," they said. "Go to Jesus."

When the man's hand closed around hers, Lily saw his death. She saw him in an alley in winter, curled up with an empty bottle at his side. Yet she gripped his fingers even more tightly as he led her down the rows of bleachers, onto the dirt floor, and out of the tent.

• TWELVE •

"CHRIST, THIS BASTARD gets heavier every night."

Baba Yaga held tightly to one of the four ropes that lowered the platform upon which Reverend Silas Everyman descended to the stage. To her the weight was nothing, but the other three handlers were groaning with the effort of keeping an even tension on the guide lines.

"Letting him down is the

easy part," said another of the men. "Just wait until we have to haul him up again at the end of the night."

When the platform was down and the Reverend had begun his performance, they let go of the ropes and went about other business. Baba Yaga stayed where she was, in an area just behind the curtain that separated the stage from the back of the tent. There she could hear every word spoken by the preacher and watch the many people who scurried about keeping the show going.

Thanks to the fortune teller, she also now had a better understanding of Jesus, and so when Everyman invoked his name, she listened. In her lifetime she had heard many gods invoked. Sometimes they came, but more often they didn't. She waited to see what this one would do. She felt nothing, but the crowd on the other side of the curtain seemed to believe that he had come among them. She considered the possibility that he revealed himself only to the devout. There were some who did that, although in her experience they were generally tricksters masquerading as something more, afraid to show themselves to anyone who might be skeptical of their true nature.

"Well, it's showtime."

Baba Yaga looked at the person standing beside her. It was unmistakably a woman's voice she'd heard, yet the presence of an impressive beard on the speaker's face suggested otherwise. Having whiskers herself, however, Baba Yaga was less concerned with this than she might have been.

She watched as the woman went onstage, then listened with interest as the preacher described her alleged sins. When the woman passed back through the curtain, Baba Yaga asked, "Is any of it true?"

The woman laughed. "Only if you believe a child is capable of sin," she said. "My beard began growing when I was only four."

"Why do you let him say those things about you?"

"It's this or Bingham & Broadley's Circus of Mystery," the woman answered. "And he offered me more than they did."

Baba Yaga said nothing. She watched as others passed through the curtain and onto the stage, listened as their failings were enumerated by Everyman. She heard the murmurings and gasps of the crowd, and felt the change in the air when the preacher once again uttered the name of Jesus.

Yes, there was something here. A presence. Something powerful conjured up by the man commanding the stage. Baba Yaga was impressed by his abilities. But what he had called into the tent remained a mystery to her. He named it Jesus. Lord. God. But it was none of those things. It was something both less and more.

"What are you?" Baba Yaga whispered. "Why won't you show yourself to me?"

She waited for an answer. None came. But Baba Yaga could wait. She had outwaited mountains and kingdoms. And so she seated herself on a wooden crate and waited until it was time to pull the ropes again.

• THIRTEEN •

OUTSIDE, THE AIR WAS cooler, and Lily realized how hot she had felt inside the tent. It was as though her skin were on fire. As the clown led her away from the big top, she heard Reverend Everyman's voice muffled by the sounds of cheering. As soon as she could, she let go of the messenger's hand and wiped her palm on her dress, as though somehow that would wash away the vision of his death, which remained in her mind like dirt on her skin.

Without a word, she followed him into another, smaller tent. This one was filled with tables and chairs. The men in clown suits sat on one side of the tables, while across from them sat the people they had led from the meeting. Everyone spoke very quietly, and the air crackled with whispers so that it sounded like the summer night right before a thunderstorm.

The man led Lily to a table in a corner of the tent and sat down. She took the chair opposite him, fixed her gaze on his whitened face with its large circles around the eyes, and waited for him to speak. Now that she was away from the crowd, she felt a little bit silly, and didn't know what was expected of her.

The man rested his hands on the table and smiled, his big red mouth curling up like the edges of a dying rose petal. Despite his smile, his eyes were dull, and Lily found herself wondering what events in his life would take him from the world of the tents to his violent death on an abandoned street.

"Why did you answer the call?" he said flatly.

Lily thought for a moment. She really didn't know why she had done it. When Everyman had been speaking, he seemed to be speaking directly to her. He seemed to Lily to know exactly how she felt inside her heart. But now that she was seated across from someone asking her to explain what she'd felt, she found that she couldn't. She shook her head. "I don't know," she said.

The man looked around and sighed. "Is it because you're a sinner?" he asked without interest. "Do you feel the touch of sin in your life?"

Lily nodded. "Yes," she said simply. "I'm a sinner." While she couldn't tell the man why she felt this, she knew that it was true.

"How have you sinned?" he went on. "Have you taken the Lord's name in vain? Have you had evil thoughts? Have you given in to lust?" He licked his lips, the tip of his tongue protruding as if he were waiting to taste her answer.

"I've killed," Lily said simply.

The man looked at her. "Killed?" he said, puzzled. "You mean you've killed an insect, or a mouse. Maybe a cat?"

Lily shook her head. "I killed my father," she said.

The man glanced around the room. He leaned back in his chair and tapped on the table. "What do you mean you killed your father?" he said.

"I touched him, and he died," Lily explained. "Now everyone I touch dies. I see them dead. It's because of sin. I can feel it inside me."

The man wiped his hand across his forehead. "Where is your mother?" he asked. "Are you alone?"

"I don't know where she is," Lily answered. "I came to see Reverend Everyman. Someone told me he has magic in his hands. Like I do. Only his magic heals, and mine kills. That's sin, isn't it?"

The man was staring at her, and Lily could see that he was afraid. She wondered if, like some of the others, he could see the other girl inside of her. She decided that she should leave, and stood up.

"I'm sorry," she said, and stood.

The man jumped up. "Wait!" he said. "Please, wait here. I'm going to get someone who can help you." He grinned nervously at her, as though he were looking at a dangerous dog. She felt sorry for him, so she sat back down. The man ran out of the tent, almost tripping in his haste to leave.

A few minutes later, the man returned. He had with him another man, who was short and very thin. He was dressed in a black suit that wrapped his body like a shroud, and his face was pinched. A pair of gold-rimmed glasses perched on his nose like a weathervane on a dilapidated barn roof, and his hair was combed over one side of his head. The clown was speaking to him and gesturing toward Lily.

The man approached the table and sat down. He looked at her

silently for a few minutes, then spoke in a voice like a flame being blown out. "Hello, young lady," he said. "I am Mr. Sims. Edgar there tells me that you have something you'd like to talk about."

Lily's throat was dry. The calmness she had felt inside the tent with Silas Everyman had vanished under the gaze of the strange man who peered at her as though she were a painting on a wall. His voice floated on the air like smoke, and it made her feel like choking. She pressed her back against the chair and tried to remain calm.

"My name is Lily," she said. "I killed my father. I have sin in my hands." She held her hands up for the man's inspection. It was the first time she had called the power inside her by this new name, and it made her ashamed.

Mr. Sims regarded her with a look of both puzzlement and amusement. He leaned back in his chair and took a deep breath. "Young lady," he said gently. "I don't know what happened to your father, but I'm sure you're a very good little girl. You do not —"

"I see death," Lily interrupted. "I see death through my hands and it comes true."

Mr. Sims sighed. "Look," he said. "If you would like me to pray with you, I would be more than happy —"

Something inside Lily snapped. She knew that Sims didn't believe her. Reaching across the table, she grabbed his wrist and closed her fingers around it. Instantly, she saw him in a bed, alone in a dark, damp room. His skin was shrunken around his bones, and he looked like a skeleton wrapped in tissue paper. She knew that he had died of something that had taken its time eating away at him from the inside.

"Cancer," she said, the word coming to her from deep in her throat. "You will die of it. In two years. Already it is in you."

She let go of Sims's hand and sat back in her chair. He was holding his wrist with his other hand, rubbing it as if in pain. On his face was a look of utter astonishment.

"H-How do you know that?" He looked frightened. His hand trembled. "How do you know?"

"I saw you. I saw you dead, and then the word for it came to me. It is true, isn't it?"

Sims looked down, but he didn't answer her. After a moment, he looked up. His eyes were wet with tears. "You'd better come with me," he said. He stood up, smoothed his suit, and motioned for Lily to follow him.

"Will you be able to help me?" Lily asked as they left the tent and began to walk through the rows of smaller tents. "Can you take the sin away?"

Sims didn't answer her as he turned a corner and headed for an all-white tent set apart from the others. A large man stood near the entrance, and he nodded at Sims as they entered. He glanced at Lily, then snapped his eyes straight ahead once more.

When they were inside, Sims pointed to a chair and told Lily to sit down.

"What am I waiting for?" Lily asked him, sitting down.

Sims hesitated, looking at her over his shoulder. "For the Reverend."

Before Lily could ask another question, he ducked through the tent opening and was gone. Lily saw the shadow of the guard move to block the only way out, his broad back looming against the whiteness of the wall.

The chair was uncomfortable. The wooden seat was hard, and the ground upon which the tent was pitched was uneven, so that every time she moved, the legs of the chair wobbled. Despite this, she didn't get up. Instead, she tried to keep perfectly still. She closed her eyes and breathed in the hot, dry air. The tent smelled of dust, and Lily found herself wondering if this is what it felt like to lie in a coffin.

She opened her eyes. Outside, people were passing by the tent in both directions. Their shadows were reflected on the cloth walls, and their murmured voices came and went. Sometimes they laughed or called out "Hallelujah!" This made Lily feel more hopeful, although she couldn't say why.

She wondered what Revered Everyman would think of her. More, she wondered if he could truly help her. She hoped that he could, that he could remove or stop or banish the thing inside her. Maybe then, her mother wouldn't fear her. Maybe then, they could return home.

She sat for a long time. One leg went to sleep, and she pinched the skin of her calf to wake it. Finally, the tent flap opened again and the Reverend entered, followed by Sims. He stopped in front of the chair in which Lily sat and looked at her for a moment. Then he smiled widely. "Mr. Sims tells me that you need my help," he said.

Lily nodded. "Can you take the sin out?" she asked.

The Reverend laughed. "Now, what makes you think you need me to do that?" he asked.

"I can feel it," she said. "Inside of me. It's growing. She's growing."

Everyman's eyebrows raised. His brow furrowed. "She?"

"The girl who calls death to her," said Lily. She glanced at Sims. "I showed him."

"Yes, he told me," said Everyman. "Can you do that again? Tell me how someone will die?"

Lily shook her head. "I don't want to. Every time I do, it makes her stronger. I want you to stop her. To stop it."

The Reverend nodded. "Of course," he said. "I understand. But first I need to be sure." He turned and called out, "Anna, come in here."

A woman entered the tent. Her face was not wrinkled, nor her hair gray, but to Lily she seemed somehow older than all of them. Her skin was sallow, and her hair greasy. She wore a faded, patched dress and no shoes. For a moment she stared at Lily with flat, fearful eyes, then dropped her stare back to the dirt floor.

"This is Anna," Everyman told Lily. "She works as a washer woman for the caravan. Anna, give Lily your hand."

Anna shrank back, but was urged forward by the Reverend's hand on her back. She held her hand out toward Lily. It was trembling. Lily didn't want to touch it.

"Go on," the Reverend told Lily. "It's all right. It's just a test. To make sure that you really need my help. I can't help you if I don't know for certain that you're telling the truth."

Lily, afraid that he might turn her away, raised her hand, palm up, and Anna lowered her hand to meet it. As soon as their flesh was joined, Lily's head was filled with a vision. She saw Anna bent over a tub of dirty, steaming water. Clothes floated in the tub, and Anna stirred them with a long wooden stick. Then she coughed, and spittle flew from her mouth, flecking the clothes and water with blood. The coughing continued until Anna collapsed, pulling the tub over as she fell so that the water splashed across her crumpled body. Lily pulled away. Anna, startled, put her hand to her mouth as a gasp of fear escaped her lips.

"What did you see?" Everyman asked Lily.

"Blood," said Lily, not looking at Anna. "She's coughing up blood. It's in her lungs."

There was silence as the Reverend looked at Anna. "You've never seen this girl before, is that right?"

"Never," Anna whispered.

"And what she says," Everyman continued. "It's true?"

"Yes," said Sims when Anna failed to answer. "The physician confirmed it just this morning. Anna has tuberculosis."

"You can go," the Reverend told Anna. "Sims will see to you."

The woman and Sims departed, leaving Lily alone with Everyman. He took a handkerchief from his pocket and wiped his brow. "How long have you been able to do this?" he asked. "To see how people will die."

"Not long," Lily told him. "Since my birthday."

"Who knows about this? Your mother and father? Friends? Who have you told?"

"My mother knows," Lily said. "My father is dead." She wondered why he didn't remember this.

"Anyone else?" asked Everyman.

Lily thought about Alex Henry. Should she tell the Reverend about him? Her mother had instructed her never to mention the village. "No," she said. "No one else. Until now."

The Reverend nodded. "Good. That's good."

"Is it sin?" Lily asked him. "Can you help me?"

Everyman, ignoring this, said, "Where is your mother now?"

Lily gestured toward the big tent. "Out there. Somewhere."

"We'll need to find her," said the Reverend. "You can tell Sims what she looks like when he returns. He'll take care of it."

"So you can help me?" Lily asked.

Everyman nodded. "I can. But it won't be easy. This is the Devil's work, make no mistake about it."

Lily didn't understand what he meant, but he sounded so certain that she believed him. She remembered him talking about a devil before, in regards to the girl with the marks on her skin. Was this the same? She wanted to ask, but the Reverend was talking again.

"Don't you worry. The Devil is no match for me. I've tamed him before, and I can tame him again."

"And Jesus," said Lily. "The King. He can help?"

"Of course. Of course he can. Me and Jesus, we can fix anything."

Relief flooded through Lily. She stood up, knocking the chair over, and ran toward Silas Everyman with her arms flung wide. "Thank you!"

"Stop!" the Reverend commanded.

Lily did so, standing a few feet from him and wondering what she had done wrong. He held his hands out towards her. On his face she saw an expression of fear, which a moment later changed to a smile. He chuckled gaily. "I don't want to get my suit dusty."

Lily looked down at herself and saw that she was indeed very dirty from her long day. She smiled back at the Reverend.

"All right," Everyman said. "Now, why don't you sit back down and we'll wait for Sims to come back. Then you can tell him all about your mother, and he can go find her."

"And then you'll take the sin out of me?" asked Lily.

The Reverend pointed to the chair. "You just sit right there. I'll take care of you. I promise you that."

Lily went to the chair, righted it, and sat. She placed her hands in her lap. "I'll wait right here."

"That's a good girl," said Everyman. "And here, while we're waiting you can look at this." He reached into his back pocket and pulled out a small booklet, which he tossed into Lily's lap.

"What is this?" she asked, picking it up.

"That's the Wordless Book," the Reverend told her. "It explains how sin works, and how we're going to save you."

Lily looked at the first page, which was nothing but pure black.

"That's what sin is like," Everyman said. "Just blackness. That's how you are inside. Like a night with no stars."

Lily understood this. She did feel black inside, filled with darkness and no light. But she'd also seen nights with no stars, and knew that they could be beautiful too. She was about to ask the Reverend to explain further, but he spoke first.

"Turn the page. See how it's all red? That represents the blood of Jesus Christ."

"Blood?" said Lily.

Everyman nodded. "The blood that was spilled when he was hung on the cross. Surely you know the story of how Jesus died for your sins."

Lily shook her head. "Until today, I'd never heard of Jesus the King."

"Well, we'll fix that soon enough," said the preacher. "All you need to know right now is that he died for you."

"Like an offering?" Lily asked. She knew about offerings. Her father had made them to the sea before setting out. Not that it had helped him in the end. But that was the thing about offerings — sometimes they weren't accepted. But you made them anyway, because sometimes, her father had once told her, the willingness to make them was more important than the result.

"Something like that," the Reverend agreed. "Now the next page, it's white. That's what color your soul is once Jesus washes away the sin."

Lily ran her fingers over the snow white paper. "How does he wash it away?"

Everyman cleared his throat and adjusted his tie. "He just does. Don't you worry about that right now."

The last page was yellow. Lily waited for the Reverend to explain its meaning.

"Heaven," he said. "And the crown of gold you get when you arrive there."

"Where is it?" asked Lily. "Heaven. Is it a town, like Salvation and Pilotsville?"

The reverend shook his head. "I'm going to have to have a long talk with your mother when we find her. No, Heaven is where Jesus lives, and where we go when we die if we believe in him and do what's right."

Lily shut the book. It didn't make sense to her, and she had questions, but before she could ask them, the tent flap opened again and Sims reappeared.

"Ah," said Everyman, sounding relieved. "You're back. Good. I have a job for you."

FOURTEEN

Baba Yaga picked up the book. It had been dropped by one of the clowns, and was lying in the dirt. She dusted it off and opened it to the first page.

She had seen wordless books before, of course. She had several in her library at home. Some of them contained powerful magic in the form of pictures and symbols. Others were tricks, containing words that were hidden and could only be read in the light of a full midsummer moon, or by pricking one's finger and feeding the words with blood. She recalled one that could only be read with a dying breath. It had taken her several years and the assistance of a hundred or more souls to get through that one, although now she forgot what it contained. She would have to read it again.

This book was...different. She felt no magic in it. And yet she'd seen the faces of those who looked at it transformed. Many had wept. Some had laughed. A few had fallen down as if struck dead. The clowns had consoled them as necessary, but mostly they had just smiled their painted smiles and waited to take the books back again.

She turned to the red page. What had the Reverend said about blood? Something about Jesus the King dying on a cross as an offering. Well, that was hardly new. Kings had been doing things like that forever, usually unwillingly, although she'd known a few to do it for the sake of a harvest or to curry favor with one of the gods. Sometimes it worked, although mostly it didn't. Gods were like that. But people kept trying.

What had this king died for, this Jesus? For the sins of the people? That seemed to be the message of the book, if the white page was to be believed. But this hardly made sense. Surely the people could do their own dying, were in fact doing it every second of every hour. So what was the point?

Obviously, it hadn't worked.

And why was it only kings who did such things? She'd never heard of a queen attempting it. Probably they were more sensible, or too busy. Only men had time to think of such foolishness.

Then there was the gold. Gold she could understand. Gold you could hold in your hand and count, or fashion into useful things, or use to lure the greedy into a trap. It had weight and value. Blood did too, of course, but in a different way. Gold was simpler. And it could be carried in a sack.

It made sense to her that Jesus might promise gold to those who followed him. That was a good way to win favor with people. Although if they had to die before getting the reward, that made it problematic. Or perhaps not. Perhaps it simply meant that Jesus the King never had to make good on his promise. With some interesting exceptions, the dead seldom complained about broken contracts.

She tucked the book into one of her pockets to look at later. She still had questions. But at the moment she was hungry. Hoisting the Reverend up and down had caused her to work up an appetite. She sniffed the air, found a promising scent, and set off after it, wondering if she might find an oven somewhere about, or at least a fire. Raw would do, but she preferred roasted.

• FIFTEEN •

LILY LAY ON HER BACK, looking up at the night sky. Her mother had been found, and was now talking to the Reverend Silas Everyman inside the tent. Lily had been sent outside with Mr. Sims. That had been two hours ago. She was first taken to a large tent in which people were eating. There she was seated at a table of clowns and given a bowl of soup made with vegetables and a sandwich containing cheese and meager slices of some kind of meat. Neither was particularly good, but she was hungry and so ate quickly and eagerly. The clowns did not speak to her.

Afterward, Sims brought her to a grouping of small wooden cottages on wheels. It was explained to her that the people who worked for the Holy Gospel Caravan lived in the houses — which were pulled by trucks — as they traveled from place to place. At least, the important people did. People like Sims and the Reverend himself. The others rode in buses and slept in tents.

Sims was then called away to attend to something more important, and he told Lily to stay near the wagons until he got back, and not wander off. This she was happy to do, as she was tired, and so she walked a little way behind the wagons, to the edge of a field, and made a nest of a kind by flattening the grass the way she had seen hares and foxes do.

The ground beneath her was still warm from the heat of the day, and the breeze that rippled the tall grass of the field whispered in her ears. The sounds of the carnival seemed far away, although from time to time she heard voices raised in song, and occasionally a "Hallelujah!" or "Amen!" broke the stillness.

She wondered what her mother and the Reverend were saying about her. Her mother had not looked pleased to be brought to the tent, and had frowned at Lily as if she had done something wrong. Sims had taken Lily away before she could explain, and so now Lily worried that her mother was angry with her.

She pushed the thought from her mind and concentrated on the stars, looking for familiar constellations. But the heavens looked different from what she remembered, and she became confused. Nothing was where it ought to be. She closed her eyes and tried to recall what the sky should look like.

When she opened them again, someone was standing beside her and looking down into her face. It was the old man from the fortune teller's tent. Only now as she looked at him, he appeared again to be a child. In one hand he held a lantern, the globe of which was filled with a pale, flickering light. It took Lily a moment to realize that the light came not from any flame, but from the glow of a dozen fireflies.

Lily and the boy stared at one another for a moment. The fireflies winked on and off. Then Lily said, "Did Mr. Sims send you to find me?"

"No," answered the boy. His voice seemed both old and young at the same time, which confused her once more.

"What's your name?" Lily asked him, hoping that having something by which to call him would make the question of his age less troubling.

"Ash," he answered. He sat down beside her, setting the lantern in front of him. The fireflies, as if sensing they were not needed at the moment, went dark. Ash, now a shadow beside Lily, was silent.

"I was trying to remember the names of the stars," Lily said after some time.

"They're not the same here," said Ash.

Lily wanted to ask what he meant by here. Did he know about her? Did he know about her village? If so, how? Had he been there? Or did he mean something altogether different? Perhaps he was talking about where he was from. She didn't dare ask, although she very much wanted to.

"This sky has no Poisoned Queen," Ash continued. "No White Bear or Broken Ladder."

Lily had never heard of these constellations, and she wondered in what world they existed, and in which Ash had seen them, but she said nothing. Ash pointed to the sky. "There's the Scorpion," he said. "And over there, the Dragon. But their magic is asleep, or maybe dying. This whole world is dying, I think. Or maybe it's already dead and we're all just ghosts."

"I don't think I'm a ghost," Lily told him. "Are you?"

To her surprise, Ash laughed. "I'm many things," he said. "But I don't think a ghost is one of them. Although some might disagree. Are you ready to see your mother and the preacher now?"

"I thought you said Sims didn't send you to find me?" said Lily.

"He didn't," Ash replied. "But that doesn't mean I don't know that they're ready for you."

Lily got up, brushing the grass from her dress. Ash stood as well, and picked up the lantern. The fireflies glowed, illuminating his face. He looked at Lily with eyes that seemed to her to be impossibly sad. He opened his mouth as if to say something, but just then Lily heard Sims's voice calling to her.

"I'm here!" she called over her shoulder. When she turned back to Ash, she found that he had gone. The grass was just closing behind him as he disappeared back into the field.

She ran back towards the wagons, where she found Sims waiting. Seeing her, he said, "What were you doing?"

"Looking at the stars," she told him.

Sims looked up at the sky, as if perhaps he had never noticed before that it was filled with stars. Then he turned and walked away. Lily followed as they made their way back to the tents and the sounds of people talking and singing. She wondered what time it was, and whether the Holy Gospel Caravan ever truly went to sleep.

"Does the fortune teller have a wagon?" she asked Sims as they walked.

"Fortune teller?" Sims said. "There's no fortune teller in the Caravan."

"But I saw her," said Lily. "And there's a boy with her. Ash."

Sims glanced at her, his brow furrowed. "There's no boy here with that name," he said.

"Perhaps there's an old man called that then?" Lily suggested. "A very small old man who sometimes looks like a boy?"

"No," Sims said. "I don't know what you're talking about. Maybe you saw someone who was visiting. As I said, we have no fortune teller.

The Reverend would never allow such devilry here."

Lily wanted to argue, but thought better of it. Besides, a larger question had formed in her mind. "What about me?" she said. "Isn't what I do a kind of fortune telling?"

"Yes," Sims said. Lily waited for him to continue, but he said nothing more until they were once more standing outside the tent in which Silas Everyman sat with her mother.

"Go inside," Sims instructed her.

Lily slipped through the opening. She found her mother and the Reverend seated in chairs across the table from one another. There were two glasses on the table, and a bottle between them.

"Ah," said Everyman when he saw Lily. "Here she is now."

Lily's mother looked at her, then turned her head and picked up the glass that was in front of her. She drank from it in a series of quick sips.

"Your mother and I have had a nice, long talk about you," the Reverend told Lily.

"Can you help me?" Lily asked him.

The Reverend nodded. "Yes," he said. "Your mother has agreed that you need to be under my care. You're very fortunate that she's a godly woman, and understands the peril your soul is in. It's clearly the will of Jesus that brought you here."

Lily wanted to know if it was the will of Jesus that her father had to die, as they would never have left the village but for that. But then, hadn't she been the one to kill him with her kiss? Hadn't the girl inside of her been responsible for making sure that the vision came true?

"What are you going to do?" she asked.

"It's not what I'm going to do," said the preacher. "It's what we're going to do together."

Lily didn't understand. She looked again to her mother for some kind of help, but her mother's attention was on the Reverend. She gazed at him with an expression Lily found difficult to comprehend.

"Come and sit by me," Everyman said, indicating an empty chair at the table.

Lily obeyed. The chair was hard and uncomfortable, the edge of the wooden seat cutting into the soft skin behind her knees. She fidgeted, trying to get comfortable, but nothing helped. She glanced at her mother, and saw that her mother's eyes were soft and unfocused, as if she were very tired.

Everyman smiled at Lily. Unlike her mother's eyes, his were alive with excitement. He licked his lips before continuing, covering them with a thin film of spit that glistened in the light.

"Earlier tonight," he said. "Your mother and I prayed to the Lord for guidance regarding your trouble. Fortunately for you, he has provided me with an answer. I am to be the agent of your salvation. The vessel through which he will work a miracle."

Lily didn't understand. Her mother, however, murmured "Amen" and lifted one hand up. The hand also contained her glass, which she then pressed to her lips.

"You will be saved," Everyman said. He nodded his head firmly, as if some great debate had been concluded.

"How?" Lily asked.

The Reverend stood up. He extended his arms and smiled. "By helping others," he told her. "By turning your curse into a tool for healing."

Lily still didn't understand. But she felt foolish for not grasping the meaning of the Reverend's words, and so she sat quietly, concentrating on the pain in her legs.

"What is it that every soul wants most to know," Everyman continued, "but the time and manner in which it will depart this world. And you can give them the answer to this question."

Lily couldn't imagine why anyone would want to know when they would die. "How does this help them?" she asked.

The Reverend cocked his head to the side. "How?" he said. "By giving them fair warning. So that, if possible, they can prevent it. Change how and when it will occur. Postpone it for as long as possible. And if they can't postpone it, use the time they have left to get their affairs in order, spend time with their loved ones, and atone for their sins in order to be welcomed into the arms of the Lord at the moment of their passing."

Lily, rubbing one leg against the edge of the chair, felt the skin catch on a rough spot in the wood. She pressed against it, and the jagged lip bit into her flesh. "How do you know they can change what I see?" she asked. "Isn't what I see the truth?"

Everyman nodded. "Yes," he answered. "But the truth can be changed. With enough prayer and effort. What you see is what will happen if the person does nothing, continues on as he is at this moment. But the future is not written in stone."

Lily wanted to know how he knew this. Nothing in her experience so far suggested to her that what she saw when she touched someone was merely a possibility. But she knew little of these things, and the preacher had the power of his god behind him. Perhaps he was more adept at magic than she.

"Don't you see?" he said. "You will give them a chance to change their ways. And in doing so, you will yourself atone for whatever sin has brought this affliction upon you."

"You mean it will stop?" Lily asked. "If I do this?"

Everyman lifted his hands. "The Lord will surely show you mercy," he said.

Lily moved her leg once more. A drop of blood slipped from the wound she had made and began to slide down her calf. Reaching beneath her dress, she touched her fingertip to the stickiness, then brought her hand to her face. Pressing her palms together in imitation of the Reverend when he prayed, she moved her hands closer to her face and breathed in the sharp scent of metal and earth.

Everyman, thinking Lily was overcome with joy by the Lord's benevolence, winked at her mother, who turned her eyes away and looked deeply into her almost-empty glass.

"How long will it take?" Lily asked.

The Reverend tsked her. "That is the wrong question, child," he said. "It's not for us to ask God what his timetable is. Our sole duty is to serve him until he tells us our time is through."

Lily slipped the tip of her tongue between her tented fingers, searching for the curse-tainted blood that stained her skin. She wondered if she could taste it, if it somehow altered the composition of the life that flowed through her veins and made it more bitter. What flavor did damnation have? She wondered too if she could pass it along to someone else, like a sickness that jumped to another who came too near. She considered pointing her bloodstained finger at her mother, or at Everyman, to see if it brought fear to their eyes.

Another question occurred to her. "How will they know I tell the truth?" she asked Everyman.

The preacher held up one finger. "A very good point," he said. "And one I have already considered. We will need to provide examples to satisfy their curiosity and silence their doubts. Proof. But don't you worry yourself about that. The Lord will guide my hand."

Lily understood very little, but she said nothing. She was tired. Also, hope stirred in her heart. Perhaps the Reverend was right. Perhaps she could rid herself of the curse with the help of his god.

"Tomorrow we begin," Everyman declared. "So now you need your rest. I will have a wagon prepared for you in the morning, but tonight you may stay in one of the tents. Sims will show you where to go."

Lily's mother stood, and so Lily followed suit. The cut behind her knee had clotted, but she saw that she had left blood smeared on the wood of the chair. A fly landed on the stain and began to explore with its curious feet the message left behind by her body. Lily wondered if it would die, or if perhaps it too would now see the deaths of every living thing upon which it alit. If so, would it drive the tiny creature mad, knowing such secrets?

"Say thank you." Her mother's voice hissed in her ear.

Lily looked at Everyman, who was filling his glass from the bottle. "Thank you," she said.

The preacher nodded. "We're going to do great things together," he told her. "Great things."

Lily's mother said goodnight, and she and Lily left the tent. Once more, Sims was there. He said nothing as they walked, this time heading for a field filled with tents. Unlike the small gathering of wagons, the sprawling tent city was bustling with life. Campfires burned outside some of them, while music filled the air as harmonicas, fiddles, and voices joined together. Laughter, not all of it kind, trickled between the rows of tents, and clowns moved in and out of the shadows.

"I apologize for the accommodations," Sims said as they stopped in front of a tent that resembled all of the others. "Tomorrow I will find something more suitable for you. Your arrival was of course unexpected."

"Yes," said Lily's mother. "I understand. I think we will be all right for one night."

Sims nodded and left. Lily and her mother entered the tent. Inside they found two wood-and-canvas cots covered with thin, wool blankets. There was also a battered wooden washstand, upon which sat a china basin filled with water. A cake of white soap and two cloth towels were beside it. A small trunk sat between the cots, with a lantern on it.

Lily's mother undressed, folding her stockings and her dress and laying them over the trunk. She sat on the edge of one of the cots and yawned. When she saw that Lily wasn't copying her, she asked, "What's the matter?"

"I need to make water," Lily said.

Her mother sighed. "Go out there and ask someone where to go," she said. She slipped her feet beneath the blanket of her cot and laid her head down on the pillow, closing her eyes.

Lily looked at the tent door. Beyond it was the world of the clowns and others who served the Reverend. She wished she could call for Sims to show her the way through it. The thought of walking among them alone filled her with dread, although she couldn't say precisely why that was or what she feared.

She undressed and got into her cot, trying to ignore the pressure in her belly. She closed her eyes, hoping that sleep might overtake her and make her forget the restless demands of her body, which seemed determined of late to betray her in every possible way. But the heaviness inside her continued to grow.

"Lord," she prayed silently, imitating the Reverend's words. "Help me, please." She hoped that now that she was in partnership with Everyman, she might have access to his god and his miracles.

She waited, the blanket gripped tightly in her hands. Outside, the laughter of the clowns seemed to rise up and surround the tent. And then she felt the warm rush between her legs as her prayer was answered.

• SIXTEEN •

BABA YAGA made her way through the tangle of tents, following the faint sound of dice rattling in a cup. She loved games of chance, and was in the mood to try her luck. So when she located the group of clowns huddled around a fire, throwing dice in the dirt, she joined them. None of them gave her a second glance.

"Have you seen his new pet?" one of the clowns, the one with the dice, said.

"The girl?" said another, throwing a coin onto the ground. "Is she for the show?"

"Aren't they all?" said a third. "Isn't everything for the show?"

They all laughed, including Baba Yaga. She wondered how much the clowns really knew, and how much they cared. Probably not much on both counts, she thought. She tossed a coin beside the others. It was silver, but it was not of this land. As she recalled, it was from one of the hells. But whether it was used as a token to enter or leave, she couldn't remember.

"I think he's more interested in the mother," said the first clown, casting the dice. "It's been a while since he had one his own age."

He rolled an eight. More coins were added to the pile. Baba Yaga contributed a polushka.

"One of them must have some worth," the third clown said. "He's giving them a wagon. Although tonight they're here with us."

The first clown rolled again. Eleven. Baba Yaga, who was out of coins, placed a robin's egg on the pile.

"I wonder how long until he tires of them and gives them to us," said the second clown.

The clown with the dice rolled a seven. His compatriots, who had wagered against this happening, swore their annoyance. Baba Yaga, mulling over what she had just learned, was content to let him keep what he had taken from her. Robin eggs were easy enough to find.

She left the clowns to their game and went in search of the girl, which was readily accomplished by listening to the gossiping tongues and following their path. Baba Yaga sniffed the air around the tent. The girl had pissed herself. Well, no matter. These things happened when you were afraid. And the child, she thought, should be very much afraid. Something was building, a rising of power that was sure to grow into a storm of some sort, with the girl at the center of it. She would be tested, and fiercely.

The old witch took out from a pocket the bottle she had stolen from the preacher's tent. There was only a little of the clear liquid left in it. She upended the bottle into her mouth, feeling the white fire burn its way down her throat. It reminded her of the potato vodka she made herself, but leaner and less morose.

She took another swig, and held it in her mouth for a moment before spitting it at the opening to the girl's tent. She mumbled some words, made some signs with a single bony finger, and turned away. Nothing would bother the girl for the rest of the night. Perhaps it was breaking the rules, but so be it. The child was going to have a difficult enough time as it was come morning.

• SEVENTEEN •

LILY USED THE WATER in the washbasin to wipe away the shame of the night before. Afraid to get up and light the lantern, lest she wake her mother, she had lain in her soiled cot until sheer exhaustion caused her to fall asleep. Now with dawn lightening the walls of the tent, she cleaned herself and changed into a fresh dress from her bag. She could do nothing about the cot or the blanket, and so left them as they were.

She was combing her hair when her mother stirred, yawning and stretching her arms. Her nose wrinkled, and Lily held her breath, fearful that her failure would be revealed. But her mother only yawned again and sat up. She barely glanced at Lily as she began to ready herself for the day.

"What are we supposed to do?" Lily asked after a moment.

"Wait until someone comes for us, I suppose," her mother said as she dressed. "Or go and find some coffee."

Lily glanced anxiously at the tent opening. Her mother, seeing the look of apprehension on her face, sighed. "You're going to have to get used to being here," she said. "This is our life now. No one out there is going to hurt you."

"This isn't like home," Lily said.

Her mother laughed. "No, it isn't, thank God. You're lucky I was able to get you away from that place. And remember, I told you not to talk about it."

Lily wanted to argue with her, to say that there was nothing wrong with the village. But perhaps her mother was right. After all, hadn't the curse come upon here there, the wild magic of the place infecting her? Hadn't they had to leave in order to find a way to rid her of it? There, nothing could be done. At least here she had the help of Silas Everyman.

"Come on," her mother said, running her fingers through her hair. "Enough of this nonsense."

She opened the tent flap and stepped outside. Lily's fear of following her was less than her fear of being left alone in the tent, and so she took up the bag containing the gifts from her father and went after her. Outside, the tent city was alive with activity, and once again Lily was sure that she was being watched by everyone as she walked the grassy thoroughfare. She hid her face under her hair. Her mother, ignoring the looks cast their way, walked with purpose, although Lily had no idea how she knew where they were going. To her, it all looked the same.

Somehow they found their way to a tent where food was being served. There they went through a line and collected bowls of white mush and plates with eggs and strips of fried meat. These they took to a table, where they sat and ate without speaking. Lily was also given a mug of bitter-tasting coffee, which she sipped only to wash down the oily food that settled in her stomach like sand.

As they were finishing, Sims appeared. "Here you are," he said, sounding neither pleased nor bothered. "I've been looking for you. The Reverend wants to speak with the girl."

Lily's mother wiped her hands and began to stand. "We can come right —"

"Just the girl," Sims interrupted.

Lily's mother sat. "But surely I should be with my daughter," she said.

"You will be," Sims said. "After she meets with the Reverend."

Lily's mother started to speak, then stopped. "All right," she said, forcing a smile. "Lily, go with Mr. Sims. I'll see you later."

Lily could tell from the tightness in her mother's voice that she was annoyed at being left out of whatever was happening. And part of Lily wished that her mother would come with her. But she was also relieved to be away from her for a time.

She walked with Sims out of the food tent. She wanted to speak with him, as he was the closest thing she had to a friend in this new place, but she didn't know what to say apart from asking him what the Reverend wanted with her, and she suspected that he wouldn't tell her. But then she thought of something.

"The Reverend says that people can change what I see," she said, remembering her conversation with Everyman from the day before. "With the help of his god. Perhaps he can rid you of the cancer."

Sims looked down at her. "Do you believe that?" he asked.

"The Reverend says it's so," Lily replied.

"Yes," Sims agreed. "He does."

He said nothing else, and so they walked in silence until they came once more to the tent where the Reverend was. This time, several men in suits were standing around in front of it. One of them was smoking a cigarette. When Lily and Sims approached, he nodded his head at her. "This the girl?" he asked.

"Yes," Sims answered. "Are they ready?"

"Just a minute," the man said. He stepped into the tent, and Lily heard a mumbled exchange. Then the man stepped outside and said, "She can go in. But not you. Just her."

Lily looked to Sims for reassurance. He nodded, but did not smile. Lily, suddenly afraid, hesitated.

"You don't want to keep him waiting," the man with the cigarette said, and the others laughed.

Lily entered the tent. Reverend Everyman was there, standing and talking to a man Lily had not seen before. He was tall and strongly-built, dressed in a suit similar to those worn by the men outside, although somehow he looked more imposing than they did, as if the coat and tie were holding something in. His black hair was greased back, and when he turned to look at Lily, his eyes were just as dark.

"Ah," said the Reverend. "Here she is. Lily, I want you to meet Mr. Scratch."

"Hello," Lily said.

The man regarded her with an unreadable expression, then one corner of his mouth lifted in what could have been a smile. "I hear interesting things about you," he said.

"Lily, Mr. Scratch has come for a demonstration of your abilities," the Reverend said. "Once he sees for himself what you can do, he's going to aid us in our mission."

"That remains to be seen," said Mr. Scratch.

Everyman indicated the table, at which two chairs were placed on opposite sides. "Please, Lily. Have a seat."

Lily sat. She supposed that she was to tell Mr. Scratch his future, but he remained standing. He watched her for a long moment, which made her uncomfortable, as if he was waiting for her to recite some verse or sing a song. Then, to her relief, he turned and went to the opening of the tent. He said something to the men outside, then returned.

"Leave us," he said.

Lily, thinking he meant her, started to stand. But Mr. Scratch held up a hand. "Not you," he said. "The good Reverend."

Lily looked at Everyman, who seemed taken aback.

"I want to ensure that there's no interference of any kind," Mr. Scratch said, his eyes still on Lily. "The girl will be perfectly safe."

Without a word, the preacher left the tent. Mr. Scratch then said, "In a moment, a man is going to come in. You are going to take his hand and, if what I'm told is correct, see his death. But you are not to say anything. If what you see is disturbing to you in any way, make no indication of it. He knows nothing about why he is here. When you have seen all there is to see, indicate this by releasing his hand. The man will then leave. Only then will you tell me what you've seen. Do you understand?"

Lily nodded.

"Good. Then we will begin."

He returned to the tent flap and opened it. A man entered. Like the other men and Mr. Scratch, he too wore a suit. But where theirs were clean and new and well-fitted, his was threadbare and disheveled, as if it had been washed and mended one too many times. It occurred to Lily that his face looked older than it ought to, with worry lines on the forehead and around the eyes, which were pale blue.

"Mr. Blithe, kindly take a seat across from the girl," Mr. Scratch said. "But please do not speak."

The man did as instructed. He looked at Lily, but did not smile.

"Now give her your hand," Mr. Scratch said.

Mr. Blithe extended his left hand. A thin gold band circled one finger. The nails were painfully short, as if he had been biting them. The skin on his pointer and middle fingers was yellowed.

Lily looked at Mr. Scratch, who nodded. She took a breath, reminded herself not to react to what she might see, and reached for Mr. Blithe's hand.

She was in a clearing in a wood. On the ground were three bodies: a woman in a flowered dress, a boy in dungarees and a blue-and-white checked shirt, and a girl in a pink pinafore. All three had crimson lines of blood across their throats. The girl's eyes were open, and in one hand she clutched a small stuffed rabbit.

Mr. Blithe knelt on the ground beside the woman, his hands tied behind his back. One of the men Lily had glimpsed standing outside the tent — the one with the cigarette — was behind him. One hand was on Mr. Blithe's shoulder. The other held a short, sharp-bladed knife.

As Lily watched, the man brought the knife to Mr. Blithe's throat and, with one quick motion, opened the skin. Blood flowered, spilling onto the face of the woman and spattering the front of Mr. Blithe's suit. His blue eyes looked into Lily's as he struggled for breath and, finding none, slumped forward onto the ground.

Lily fought to keep her emotions hidden as her breakfast rose in her throat and she swallowed hard. She released Mr. Blithe's hand, and the vision faded. She returned her own hand to her lap and concentrated on her breathing until her heart stilled.

"Thank you, Mr. Blithe," said Mr. Scratch. "I believe we're finished here. You may go. Mr. Fortune is waiting outside to return you to your home. Please give my regards to your family."

Mr. Blithe stood up and left. When he was gone, Mr. Scratch said to Lily, "Tell me what you saw."

Lily described the scene in the clearing. She watched Mr. Scratch's face as she spoke, to see how he reacted to her words, but he continued to look back at her with the same steady gaze. When she was finished, she waited.

"And when do you see this occurring?" Mr. Scratch asked.

"Soon," Lily answered. "It was summer in the wood, and he was wearing the suit he had on now."

"Was it difficult to keep your reaction from him?" said Mr. Scratch.

Lily nodded.

"And could you tell why he received the death he did?"

Lily shook her head. "I only see how it happens," she answered.

"So determining the level of guilt or innocence will be up to the good preacher," said Mr. Scratch. "How convenient. Now let me ask you this. Reverend Everyman believes that the deaths you see are changeable. Do you believe this as well?"

Lily considered the question. If she had warned her father, would he have stayed home instead of venturing out on the sea? Part of her wanted to believe she could have stopped him. Another — the part of her that still felt guilt over not having tried to warn him — wanted to believe that what she saw was inevitable, and that speaking of it would have changed nothing. But the Reverend's plan for her salvation required that her visions be only one possible version of what might happen, and that the future could be rewritten.

"I do," she told Mr. Scratch.

Mr. Scratch held her gaze. She grew uncomfortable. Had she answered incorrectly? She was aware that much hung in the balance regarding the accuracy of what she'd seen, and she had no reason to believe that she was mistaken in her prediction of how Mr. Blithe would meet his end. Did it also matter to Mr. Scratch whether or not she believed her visions to be only one of many possible outcomes?

"It must be terribly sad for you," Mr. Scratch said. "The people you want to touch, you can't, because either they or you are afraid of what you'll see. And the ones who will want you to touch them are also afraid, and so you will fear them in return."

He continued to look at Lily, apparently waiting for her to reply. His words chilled her, both because they were true and because she sensed that he enjoyed speaking them to her. There was no sympathy in them. If anything, his black eyes shone more brightly as he beheld her discomfort.

"Would you like to see what death waits for me?" he asked. He stepped towards her and held out a hand.

Lily looked at the well-manicured fingers, the thick wrist heavily furred with dark hair. Part of her wanted to take Mr. Scratch's hand, if only for the satisfaction of seeing that his end was an unpleasant one. She realized, with some surprise, that she hoped that he suffered. And yet, she found that she could not lift her own hand to meet his.

Mr. Scratch grinned, showing his teeth. "You're not yet angry enough at the world to want to see it destroyed," he said. "Perhaps you never will be. Time will tell."

He turned from her and walked to the entrance of the tent, passing through without another word. Lily sat alone, still unsure whether she had passed or failed the test.

A few minutes later, Silas Everyman entered, accompanied by Lily's mother. The Reverend beamed at Lily. "You did well!" he said, clearly elated.

"I don't understand how he's going to help us," Lily said. She couldn't imagine the man helping anyone.

Everyman chuckled. "Mr. Scratch is very well-connected," he said. "If he's pleased, he'll tell people about you, and they will come to us — to you — to see for themselves what it is you do. His word carries weight in many different circles."

"How do you know him?" Lily asked.

"He's a very old friend," the preacher answered, although he seemed displeased by her question.

"I don't like him," Lily said.

"Don't be rude," her mother scolded.

The Reverend smiled. "You don't have to like him," he said. "The important thing is that he likes you. Now, I have some business to attend to before the first meeting of the day. Sims will help the two of you get settled in your new accommodations, and then I hope you'll join me for the revival. We'll give Lily another day to rest before we begin her sessions with our visitors."

Everyman departed, leaving Lily alone with her mother.

"You shouldn't say such things as you did," her mother said.

"You weren't here with him," Lily told her. "You didn't see the way he looked at me."

"A great many more people are going to look at you in the days to come," said her mother. "Not all of them kindly. I told you before, you'd best get used to it."

Lily wanted to tell her mother about Mr. Blithe, and what she'd seen. But she had promised not to talk of it. Besides, her mother wouldn't care. It hurt her to admit this, but it was true. Her mother had never been warm, but now there was a coldness to her that seemed impenetrable, like the fog that sometimes obscured the forest on winter mornings. Lily supposed it was her own fault, but it stung nonetheless.

At least she's trying to help save my soul, Lily thought. *She brought me here. That's something.*

Perhaps once she had attained salvation, things would change. Perhaps then her mother would look at her differently. Perhaps then she could touch her without fear. Perhaps then they could have a home of their own. Perhaps.

She wondered what would happen next. How many hands would she have to hold, how many deaths would she have to see, before she had done enough for Everyman's god to lift the curse from her? She feared she might not be able to bear the weight of them. Each one seemed to drain a little more from her. What would happen if her strength waned before she'd completed her penance?

She closed her eyes, and immediately saw the dead face of Mr. Blithe. His eyes, still beautiful, held no life. Whatever spark it was that animated a person's body was gone from them.

Who, Lily wondered, would wrap the red cord around his chest?

• EIGHTEEN •

BABA YAGA STOOD looking down at the bodies of the Blithe family.

"I'll give you this, you're very thorough," she said to Mr. Scratch. "What did he do?"

"Unpaid debt," Mr. Scratch replied. "The usual thing."

Baba Yaga poked the body of the boy with her toe. "Seems a waste of good food," she remarked.

Mr. Scratch bent and plucked

the stuffed rabbit from the little girl's hand. He slipped it into his pocket. "You're a long way from home," he said to Baba Yaga.

Baba Yaga grunted. "It's the girl," she said. "She intrigues me." She looked at her old acquaintance out of the side of her eye. "As I think she does you."

Mr. Scratch shrugged, which told Baba Yaga that she was right. *He'll never admit finding someone else interesting,* she thought to herself. *He's too much of a narcissist.*

"Tell me about this God," she said, emphasizing the capital in an attempt to provoke him.

Another shrug. "Someone they invented," he said.

"Then he's not real?"

"Who's to say?" said Mr. Scratch. "By now he might be. They've been talking about him for a long time, perhaps long enough to make him real. I don't know. I've never met him."

Baba Yaga glanced at the bodies again. "They seem to credit you with rather a lot of things I suspect you haven't done," she remarked.

Mr. Scratch laughed. "I think blame would be a more accurate word," he said. "But it's been this way for centuries. I'm used to it." He winked. "Besides, I've done enough. I'm really not terribly nice, you know."

"An affectation," Baba Yaga said. "I've always found you delightful company."

"Only because you don't want anything from me," said Mr. Scratch. "I've yet to discover your weakness."

"I haven't any," Baba Yaga insisted. "I am perfectly content."

"And yet you left your forest to follow a child."

"That's merely boredom," Baba Yaga told him. "Besides, I haven't traveled in many years. One should travel. It's broadening. So, you're going to help the girl?"

"You're changing the subject," Mr. Scratch said.

"Only slightly," said Baba Yaga. "Well, are you?"

"I'm going to vouch for her, yes," Mr. Scratch said. "Spread the word of her abilities."

"To what end?"

"Because it entertains me."

Mr. Scratch turned and left the clearing, disappearing into the green of the woods without a farewell. Baba Yaga wasn't offended. It was just his way. Also, she knew she had vexed him, if only slightly. She cackled lowly, lest he hear her.

"He's lying," she informed the Blithe family. "You can always tell when he's lying. His left eye dims a bit. It's why he never bests me at cards."

The question on her mind was, why was he involving himself in this matter of the girl? There was something he wasn't telling her. Well, there were *many* things he wasn't telling her. But something about the girl in particular. She could understand him becoming mixed up in the game of life and death that the preacher was playing, in particular the spectator sport of watching people wrestle with their obsession over their own ends and finding ways to escape oblivion. He always enjoyed seeing them tremble in the face of their mortality.

But he could do that at any time without assistance. Death occurred with every tick and every tock. No, there was something more here that had caught his attention. Much as hers had been caught.

Well, she could wait for an answer. Truthfully, she wasn't sure why she was so intrigued herself. So why should he know? Maybe they would find out together.

She bent down and fished in the pockets of Mr. Blithe, finding only a key and a small gold cross on a chain. The cross she tossed aside, but the key she put into her own pocket. You never knew when you might need to unlock a door.

• NINETEEN •

THE HOLY GOSPEL Caravan travelled mostly at night. Reverend Everyman preferred to arrive in a new location in the early hours of dawn, so that the big top was raised, flags flying, when the townspeople awoke. Of course, posters advertising the event had already been up for days (and sometimes weeks) ahead of time, and his arrival was anticipated. Still, he liked to create the illusion of a miracle, as if the revival had dropped out of heaven while the world slumbered.

This meant that Lily had to learn to sleep while the wagon in which she and her mother now resided was pulled along by a truck. Their beds were built into the sides, to prevent them from moving about, and it was rather like being in a boat, particularly when the road was more dirt than pavement. The first night, Lily dozed fitfully, jolting awake whenever the driver of the truck (a man named Lester, who during the day worked as one of the white-faced clowns) failed to avoid a rut or hole.

Fortunately, once in place, they generally stayed there for up to a week, and then the wagon seemed more like a home than a conveyance. Not that Lily saw all that much of it. Her time was mostly spent in the small tent that the Reverend had erected especially for her. Inside of it was a tall box, made of wood and painted white, that contained a small table and chair. A small hole was cut in the front, level with the tabletop, and another was cut in the wall to the right of the chair.

Lily entered the box through a door in the back. Seated at the table, she would wait until a hand was thrust through the opening. Then she would take it and perform her task, after which she would whisper what she saw into the hole to her right. Outside, his ear pressed to this same hole, was the Reverend. It was he who delivered the news to the querent.

Lily was not privy to these discussions. They took place elsewhere, out of her hearing. Her job was simply to report her visions. It was done in this way, the Reverend told her, to shield her from any unpleasant reactions on the part of the people who came to her. Also, he said, because he needed time to consult with God to determine what penance was necessary to change any unfortunate outcomes to which she bore witness.

Although separated from them by a wall, Lily still saw the faces of those who sat across from her. As she held their hands, she saw their vision-selves ravaged by disease and ill-living, broken by violence, and felled by their own hands. Much more rarely, she saw them pass peacefully.

These deaths were a comfort compared to the others, which exhausted and saddened her.

She dutifully passed along each story to Everyman, relieved to have the responsibility for sharing them rest on his shoulders. Even so, the encounters drained her, and after the third or fourth in a day, she found it more and more taxing. She was thankful for the hours when no one came to her and she could open the door at the rear of the box and step out, although she still had to remain inside the tent. The Reverend had positioned a clown outside the entrance, and when anyone approached for a reading, he would honk a horn to alert her to the fact that she needed to secret herself inside the closet.

Twice she had been awakened in the middle of the night to provide her services. On the first occasion, the hand she took belonged to an elderly woman, surely already past her eightieth year. Lily had seen her strangled in her bed, her long hair used as a noose to choke the life from her. The second sitting had been for a man whose face was the first that Lily could not see in her vision, as it was covered by a sack made of coarse cloth. He too had a noose about his neck, although his was an ordinary rope that hung from a gallows inside a prison. The man's hands were tied behind his back, and a group of spectators seated in chairs witnessed his death throes along with Lily.

Lily had no idea how the women and men who came to her were selected. Every day she sat in the big top, listening to Reverend Everyman preach, and yet he never spoke of her or invited his audience to partake of her services. Her tent was set on the edge of the larger carnival, away from the main alleyways, and no one would stumble upon it by accident. Those who came there had to do so purposefully. But how they knew she was there remained a mystery.

She did inquire. One night, after seeing the particularly odd and disturbing death of a man who leapt from the top of a building while engulfed in flames (the building itself was untouched), she asked the Reverend how those who visited the tent happened to be there. His answer — "The Lord guides them as he guides you" — was unsatisfying, but Lily did not press for further explanation.

Nor did she ask Everyman how much closer she herself was to salvation. She wondered sometimes what the worth of each vision was, how much debt she was paying off every time she took another hand in her own. She felt no different, but she was afraid to say so. Instead, she waited to be informed of her progress. The preacher seemed pleased with her, and she considered that a good sign. She decided that when she had done enough, he would let her know.

When she wasn't in service, she was allowed to roam the carnival as she liked. However, the clowns frightened her, and it was difficult to walk amongst the crowds without accidentally touching someone and becoming trapped inside a vision, and so she largely confined herself to the big top, where she could sit in the stands and listen to Everyman preach.

She thought that perhaps she was starting to understand more about his god, if only a little. The preacher had given her another book, this one with words. He said they were the words of his god, and that she should read them and learn from them. In the quiet times during the day, and in her bed at night, she pored over the pages in search of meaning. Mostly, she didn't find it. The stories were often confusing, sometimes boring, and she was left with more questions than answers. The Reverend had little time to answer these, and her mother told her to try harder to understand things for herself.

But sometimes, while reading the book, she caught fleeting glimpses of him. She discovered amongst its pages a group of poems, and returned to them again and again. Although their meaning was seldom any clearer than that of the other passages, she loved reading them. Occasionally, a line or two would speak to her.

He heals the brokenhearted
And binds up their wounds.
He counts the number of the stars;
He gives names to all of them.

She read these words while sitting atop the wagon in the middle of the night. Unable to sleep, she'd climbed up there with the book and a lantern. Once more she'd been saddened by not being able to find the constellations from the sky over her village. At this time of the year, she should have been able to see the Dancing Girl and the Stag with the Moon in His Horns right above her. But the girl was nowhere to be found, and the stag failed to appear. Then she'd opened the book to a random page and discovered those words.

The passage reminded her of Alex Henry and his hands that healed, and once more her heart broke. At the same time, she felt a glimmer of hope. Did Everyman's god really name the stars in this world? And could he heal her heart? She needed to believe that he could. If there was no magic in this place (and she had yet to find any) then she required some other kind of assistance.

She read more from the book, looking for clues, but found nothing else. Still unready for sleep, however, she decided to walk through the carnival. At this hour, the clowns were abed, and even those visitors who remained following the evening service for further assistance from Everyman or one of his helpers would be long gone. Lily was now less afraid of who might see her and what they might think than she had been. Besides, the moon was bright and now she knew her way and how to get back to the safety of the wagon should she need to.

She walked slowly. With no destination in mind, she had no cause to hurry. Instead, she thought about Everyman's god, and Alex Henry, and wondered what was happening at that moment in the village she had left behind. It was starting to seem so long ago, although she knew that it had been only a little more than three weeks. Three weeks since she had last heard the sea. Three weeks since she had slept in her little room at the top of the house. Three weeks since she had crossed the bridge, leaving her father behind.

Very few people were out. She saw only a handful of the women who came at night to clean up after the departed visitors. They trudged along with their sacks of refuse, paying no attention to anything but the discarded paper flowers and ant-covered tufts of cotton candy they collected from the grass. None of them took any notice of Lily.

Then, passing by a tent, she heard a noise like the buzzing of bees. Curious, she peeled back the flap and peered inside. In the middle of the tent was a table, and lying on it on her stomach was the daughter of the witch — the girl with the strange black symbols on her skin. Lily saw her twice a day in the Reverend's shows, but had never seen her outside of the big top.

Four clowns held her in place, two of them pinning her arms and two holding her by the ankles. A fourth man, not a clown, stood over her. He held in his hand a device attached to a cord. It was this machine that emitted the buzzing sound.

"Hold her still," the man instructed the clowns. "If she moves, the lines will be crooked."

"What difference does it make?" asked one of the clowns as the struggling girl attempted to kick him. "Just mark her."

The man with the device lowered it to the girl's back and made several small movements. The girl cursed loudly and arched her back. The clowns laughed.

"Don't you like being tickled?" one of them asked her.

"Go to hell!" the girl shouted, and spat.

The man working on her back pushed down roughly on her shoulders with one hand and continued his work with the other. Lily could see that he was leaving marks on her skin, thick black lines that looked very much like the other designs that were already there. The ones that Everyman said had been made by demons.

"Bastard!" the girl hissed.

Lily didn't understand what was happening, but she could tell that the girl was in pain. The buzzing grew louder as the man continued to work on her. Now Lily saw blood running down the girl's side.

"Keep still!" one of the clowns ordered. "Unless you want something to happen to your sister."

The girl quieted instantly, although her breathing was still fierce.

"Ah," said a clown. "That did the trick."

"Where is she?" the girl asked, her voice filled with worry. "When can I see her?"

"When the Reverend decides that you've been a good girl," one of the clowns said. "Have you been a good girl?"

The others laughed. One of the clowns touched the girl's hair. "Have you been good?" he repeated.

The girl said nothing. Her back moved up and down, as if she were crying, but no words came out of her mouth. Still, she lay quietly as the man with the buzzing machine did his work.

Lily felt someone touch her. Instinctively, she moved away. Then, to her surprise, she realized that no vision of death was in her head. When she turned around, she saw Ash standing behind her.

"Come away from here," he said.

He walked away. Lily, with a last look at the girl, followed after him.

"What are they doing to her?" she asked.

"Marking her," said Ash.

"The Reverend says that she's marked because of her mother's sin," said Lily. "He says those are the marks of a devil."

"The only sin her mother committed was refusing to do what the preacher demanded," Ash replied. "Those marks were made by man. There are worse things in this world than devils."

Lily wanted to ask what the girl's mother had refused, and what had become of her, but she was troubled by the way Ash spoke about Everyman, as if he were to blame for what she'd seen happening to the girl. And so she said instead, "The Reverend says that you and the card reader aren't part of the Caravan."

"We're as much a part of it as he is and you are," Ash said, not unkindly.

They walked until they came to the midway. The handful of pleasure rides that accompanied the Caravan and provided amusement for its visitors were shut down for the night, their generators silenced and their lights dimmed. So Lily was surprised when Ash approached the Wheel in the Sky and opened the door to the bottommost car. He gestured for Lily to get in.

She climbed in and sat down. Ash sat beside her. A moment later, gears turned somewhere in the ride's innards and the wheel began to move, soundlessly lifting the car up. Lily gasped.

"How are you doing this?" she asked Ash.

"It's machinery," said Ash. "It wants to be useful. I simply ask it to do what it was made to do."

The Wheel in the Sky was not terribly big. None of the rides were, as they had to be able to be transported from place to place. Nevertheless, it was the second tallest structure in the carnival. Only the big top rose higher in the sky. When the car in which Lily and Ash sat came to rest at the very top of the circle, it therefore looked out over the tops of the tents. Lily could see as far as the small group of wagons, where she had left her mother sleeping.

They sat, swinging gently in the night air. Then Ash spoke.

"Again, the devil taketh him up into an exceeding high mountain, and showeth him all the kingdoms of the world, and the glory of them; and saith unto him, All these things will I give thee, if thou wilt fall down and worship me."

"Who did the devil say that to?" Lily asked him.

"To the Reverend's god," said Ash. "It's in the book he gave you."

"I haven't read all of it yet," Lily admitted. "Why did he do that?"

"Pride," Ash said. "He wanted to be adored above all things."

Lily thought for a moment. "But didn't this god create the world and everything in it?" she asked, remembering both what she had read and what she had heard the Reverend say. "How was it the devil's to give him?"

"A good question," Ash told her. "You should ask it of the Reverend one of these days."

Lily added it to the list of other questions she had yet to ask or have answered. Then she asked one of Ash. "Do you have a god in your world?"

"No," said Ash. "We have a queen. A king too, but he's of little consequence. He mainly acts as an escort at balls. And the kings don't tend to last very long anyway."

"Why is that?" Lily asked.

"The queen changes her mind," said Ash.

"Are you afraid of her?"

"Me?" said Ash. "No. The worst that could be done to me has already been done. But those who still live in my world do. She has a habit of turning her disobedient subjects into hares, and she's a fair shot with a bow."

They sat in silence for a time. Then Ash said, "I can send you home. It would take a great effort to open the door, but I will do it if you like."

Lily looked at him. His eyes were old tonight. "Why would you do that for me?"

"Because I know what it's like to be taken away from your world," he said.

"Can you not return to yours?" Lily asked him.

"Not unless the one I was exchanged for is brought back," he told her. "And I suspect he's long dead. As I said, the queen's favor is fleeting. She probably tired of his blue eyes and flaxen hair before he was even weaned."

"How long have you been gone?"

Ash shrugged. "A few days. A few hundred years. It's all the same. Do you want me to help you go back?"

Lily considered the question. She did miss her home. And there were so many things she didn't understand about the place she was in. At the same time, she still believed that Reverend Everyman and his god were her best hope of salvation. If she went home, the opportunity to rid herself of her curse might be lost forever.

"Thank you," she said to Ash. "But I think I need to stay. For now."

"I won't ask again," Ash told her. "Once you refuse, the door remains closed."

Lily shut her eyes and breathed in. The air smelled like burnt sugar, dirt, and grease. She missed the scent of the sea. But she couldn't go back. Not yet. She had come there for a purpose, and she had yet to fulfill it.

"I'm certain," she said.

"Very well," said Ash.

The Wheel in the Sky turned once more, and they descended like the sun setting behind the world.

• TWENTY •

BABA YAGA SAT IN front of the dusty, cracked mirror and contemplated her reflection. It had been many years since she had seen her own face, apart from the occasional glimpse in a lake or on the blade of a knife. Once she had been delighted to find a spoon winking at her, until she realized it was her own eye cradled in the polished bowl. Other than those few occasions, she had quite forgotten what she looked like.

It's no wonder they scream, she thought as she considered her features. Her nose strived mightily to reach her chin, and crooked first to one side and then the other. The chin it came near to meeting was itself gloriously warted; her teeth were arranged like mossy stumps in a clearing. One earlobe was missing a jagged chunk, lost, as she recalled, to a fox, or possibly the sword of a seventh son who soon found himself made into a stew without even the consolation of receiving a kiss from the princess he had come to rescue. (The princess had made a very satisfactory sausage.) Her hair contained bits and pieces of her beloved forest: twigs, several fir cones, a toadstool, feathers, and three salamanders who were forever singeing her eyebrows with their fires. As to her eyes, she supposed the less inventive storytellers would compare them to new moons, stones, or bottomless wells. Really, they were simply black, which as far as she was concerned was more than good enough.

She was in the clowns' dressing tent. Arrayed in front of her were the pots of makeup they used to paint their faces. She took one up, opened it, and dipped a dirt-streaked fingernail into it. She applied the nail to her skin, leaving behind a smear of white. It reminded her of being shat on by a finch, which amused her, and so she added more.

It took two whole pots to cover her face. One for her nose alone. She then added red spots to her cheeks and mouth, and blue around her eyes. She was admittedly careless about the whole undertaking, and the finished result was ghastly. She cackled happily and grinned, mimicking the expressions of the clowns.

Horrible, she thought, and cackled again.

Strewn about the tabletop were any number of the paper flowers the clowns handed out to visitors to the carnival. Baba Yaga picked up a white rose and twirled it in her fingers. She mimed presenting it to someone — a child, perhaps.

"The flower of salvation," she said. But her heart wasn't in it, and she sounded insincere. She tossed the flower aside with a sigh. She was bored.

A man came in and sat down at the table next to her.

"I haven't seen you before, have I?" he asked.

"I rather doubt it," said Baba Yaga. "But perhaps. Are you the youngest of three brothers? Did you catch the firebird and pluck its tail feather? Were you born out of a black hen's egg to a mother far too old to bear a child?"

The man looked at the empty paint pots. "No."

"Well then," said Baba Yaga. "It's unlikely."

The man found a pot that still contained white paint and began to make up his face. "Is this your first time with the Caravan?" he asked.

Baba Yaga was pleased to have discovered a conversation starter. "Yes. And you?"

"Second," said the man. "I did it for a summer two years ago. Then I got into some trouble in Florida and spent some time on the farm. When I got out, I looked up Everyman and he gave me my job back."

"How benevolent," Baba Yaga remarked.

The man — now almost a clown — frowned. "I don't know anything about his politics. But a job's a job. And the preacher, he don't care about what you done before, you know?"

"I do now," said Baba Yaga. She leaned over. "Just what is it you did?"

The man applied some red to his lips. "This and that. You know how it is."

"I don't," Baba Yaga said. "Tell me."

The man finished applying his makeup. "Sometimes it's better not to know too much about a person," he said. "Prevents misunderstandings."

Baba Yaga shrugged. "Suit yourself."

"We all gots our stories," the man continued after a moment. "The Reverend only hires men with stories. I'm sure you have one too, just like me."

"Oh," said Baba Yaga with a wide grin. "Yes, of course. I'm practically a book."

The man pointed a finger at her. "Exactly what I mean. And I bet you wouldn't want no one reading your book now, would you?"

Baba Yaga snorted. It seemed the only answer that wouldn't be contrary.

"That's what I like about the Reverend," the man continued. "He shuts that book and don't make you open it again. You just go on and start a new one."

He was finished with his makeup. His face floated in the mirror beside Baba Yaga's.

"Now we might as well be brothers," he said. "That's another thing I like about this job. There's a hundred other men who look just like you. Makes a guy feel part of something."

Baba Yaga winked. "And it makes it difficult to know who to blame," she said. She picked up a paper flower and extended it toward the man. "The flower of salvation?"

The man took it from her. "Amen, brother," he said. "Amen."

TWENTY ONE

ON THE FINAL NIGHT before leaving each town, Reverend Everyman held a baptism for the newly-saved. For these occasions he had built a large tank, complete with a glass window in the front, which would be wheeled onstage and placed beneath a spotlight. Steps were built into each side, and the unbaptized lined up on stage right where, one at a time, they descended into the tank, where the Reverend awaited them dressed in a white suit.

Unlike the preacher, the participants were unclothed. This was required because, according to Everyman, it was imperative that sinners enter into the waters of salvation as newborn children, having discarded their sinful outer selves in preparation for being cleansed by the healing touch of God. And so those awaiting their turns stood, hands covering themselves as best they could, until it was time for the clowns to hand them down.

Once in the tank, the man, woman, or child would stand while the Reverend said, "Verily, verily, I say unto thee, Except a man be born of water and of the Spirit, he cannot enter into the kingdom of God." He would then ask three questions.

"Do you admit your sins before God?"

"Do you ask his forgiveness?"

"Do you accept his gift of everlasting life?"

Once the acceptable answers were given, the sinner was then dipped backward, supported on Everyman's arm, into the water. After a moment, they were raised up and helped up the stairs on the opposite side of the tank, where they were wrapped in a white robe and escorted off stage.

Two nights after seeing the witch's daughter being marked, Lily sat in the big top and watched as the baptism unfolded. It had been a typically successful week of preaching, and the stage was crowded with the soon-to-be-reborn. She found it interesting to watch them as they waited, particularly the families. Her eyes were drawn to a mother, father, and three boys who were standing amidst a group of single bodies. The smallest boy, five or six years old, stood with his hands on his hips, craning his neck to watch those going before him get plunged into the water. Each time one ascended the far side, he lifted his little hands and shouted "Hallelujah!" along with the Reverend, jumping up and down excitedly. His older brothers, twice his age, showed no such enthusiasm, covering themselves with their big, bony hands and looking down at their feet. Their parents, standing behind them, had their eyes closed and their hands lifted up.

Throughout the baptism, a choir arranged on risers behind the tank sang hymns. The choirs were invited from local churches in each town, and being asked to perform for the Holy Gospel Caravan was a much-coveted honor amongst the singers, each of whom gave their all for the Reverend's shows. While during the week they sang all manner of hymns and spirituals, during the baptism they all sang the same song. As Everyman asked his three questions, they hummed wordlessly, but as each dedicant was raised from the baptismal waters, they sang:

"As I went down in the river to pray,
studying about the good old way.
Who shall wear the starry crown?
Good Lord, show me the way."

The choice was deliberate. Along with being clothed in a white robe, each person exiting the tank received a crown. Made of paper to which shiny gold stars were glued, they were piled in a bushel basket off to one side. The clown assisting people down the stairs to the stage placed one on each head. They sparkled under the lights.

Lily knew that both the robes and crowns were returned once the freshly-baptized were backstage, although they were allowed to keep the crowns if they deposited a sufficient number of coins in the collection box under the watchful eye of one of the clowns. Many did. Lily wondered if they wore them once they were home.

Although she found the singing uplifting, the actual baptisms frightened her. They were too much like drowning. Sometimes the person dunked beneath the water would panic, thrashing about and pressing their hands against the glass until they were rescued by

Everyman raising them up again. Occasionally, particularly with the smaller children, they would simply swim across, limbs paddling like a dog's, while the people watching from the stands applauded.

Despite the feelings it roused in her, Lily watched each baptism closely, her eyes fixed on the glass to see if she could witness the exact moment when grace was bestowed by Everyman's god and the sinner was transformed. Was it when the water closed over the head? When the Reverend proclaimed the hallelujah that accompanied each emergence? She didn't know.

She saw joy in the faces of those exiting the tank. And there were many tears. Still, she wondered when and how the change occurred. She never questioned the use of water. Everyone knew that water could dispel any number of troublesome things. So it made sense to her that it would be involved, particularly as the other element useful for such things — fire — would be unsuitable. But the mechanics of the thing eluded her.

Only once had she seen someone resist. A girl of four or five. At first, when she refused to enter the tank of her own accord, Lily (and everyone else) had assumed that she was simply afraid of the water. But then her mother had attempted to carry her in, and the girl had begun screaming and beating her mother about the face. Even the Reverend had been unable to control her, and had ended up with a bloody nose after one of her kicking feet landed a blow to his face. Then the choir had ceased its singing, and he had ordered the mother out of the tank. Lily, staring at the pink cloud that had formed in the water, had been both horrified and somewhat thrilled by the disobedience. Everyman, after the few minutes it took to stop the bleeding, made a comment about sparing the rod spoiling the child, and then carried on.

The baptism services went on for a long time, and to keep the audience alert, the clowns passed out cotton candy. Lily had developed a taste for it, and now she sat holding a paper cone topped by a bright blue puff of spun sugar. As she watched the procession of people enter and exit the tank, she picked off bits of the fluff and put them in her mouth, where they dissolved on her tongue.

As the choir serenaded him, the little boy she had been watching clambered up the stairs and, before the clown could assist him, flung himself into the tank. His brothers, waiting their turns, shook their heads, while his parents beamed. The Reverend, laughing, caught the boy up in his arms and lifted him up so that everyone could see his smiling face.

"Do you admit your sins before God?" he asked.

The boy shrieked and trembled.

"Do you ask his forgiveness?"

"Yes!" He clapped his little hands.

"Do you accept his gift of everlasting life?"

"Yes!"

Before the boy could say anything else, Everyman plunged him into the water, shouting, "I baptize you in the name of the Father, the Son, and the Holy Ghost!"

Lily, who was watching the boy through the glass, saw him open his mouth. Bubbles streamed out. He appeared to be laughing. Was this, she wondered, the moment she had been waiting to see? Even now, was the preacher's god performing a miracle on the tiny believer? She strained forward, the ball of cotton candy she had just plucked off sticking her fingers together.

The preacher lifted the boy from the water, and the choir broke into song. But instead of joyously splashing to the other side, the child lay limply in Everyman's arms. The Reverend looked down at him, perplexed. He jounced the boy, whose mouth opened and water trickled out. A momentary expression of panic flashed across the preacher's face. "This child has been overcome by the Spirit!"

He handed the boy to one of the clowns, whispering something inaudible to the audience. The clown took the child and hurried off into the shadows of the stage.

Lily looked at the boy's family. His brothers were looking at one another with frightened expressions. His parents, however, were raising their hands and calling "Amen!" along with the choir. The mother urged one of the older boys forward and up the steps.

Lily slipped out of the stands, dropping what was left of her cotton candy in a trash barrel as she exited the big top. She walked around it to the back of the tent, where several trucks were parked in preparation for the tear-down that would come as soon as the show was over. There she discovered five clowns standing around the body of the boy, who had been laid down on the grass.

He wasn't moving. His eyes, which were open, stared up at the sky, as if he were searching for the face of God in the stars. His chest did not rise.

Lily, looking at him, saw her father lying on the beach. Before she could think better of it, she rushed to the boy's side, dropping to her knees in the grass and snatching up his hand. It was cold. But she wasn't in search of a pulse. She wished to see if this was indeed his death.

She saw him as a man of fifty-seven. He was lying in a forest while three hounds fended off a bear that was attempting to crush his head with its teeth. The bear had already mortally wounded him, tearing a gash in his belly with its claws. He in turn had shot the bear in the shoulder with his rifle, but now he was out of bullets. He would die within a few minutes.

But if that was his ordained death, what was the one he was currently in the midst of? Did it mean that someone would save him? Would his god perform a miracle? Lily looked at the clowns, who had drawn back from her and were staring impotently at one another. They would do nothing. The boy's only hope was her. But should she save him, only for him to die this other, more horrible death? Would it not be kinder to let him go?

She was inclined to think so. But then she considered all of the things the boy might experience before those final moments in the forest. Love. Children. The untold small graces and delights that comprise a life. Dying now would rob him of those things.

She bent and placed her mouth on his, pushing breath into his lungs. Her hands pressed on his chest, as she had once seen Alex Henry do to a man who had been rejected by his merfolk lover and cast back onto the beach. She repeated the actions while the boy's death as a man replayed itself over and over in her head.

The boy sputtered. Water spewed from his lips, and he blinked his eyes. Lily rocked back on her heels and watched as he coughed again, then turned his head to look at her.

"Am I redeemed?" he asked. "Did I get a crown?"

Lily nodded. "Someone will bring it to you," she said.

Then the clowns were there, rushing to pick the boy up. She knew they would return him to the big top, and that Everyman would celebrate his triumphant revival. The Lord would be praised, and more hymns would be sung. He would indeed get his starry crown and white robe, and for the rest of his life he would believe that the Holy Spirit had filled him and raised him from the dead. Even at the moment of his death, he would look at the bear that killed him and see an angel.

Lily got to her feet. Exhausted, she wanted only to go back to the wagon and collapse. But a need for answers took her back into the big top, where she waited behind the stage for the show to be over. When Everyman, his white suit streaming with the holy waters of baptism, finally left the stage and retreated to his private tent, she followed him.

"The clowns told me what you did," he said, allowing her to accompany him.

"He was dying," she informed him as he walked behind a large wardrobe trunk that stood in one corner and began to remove his sodden clothing. "But I saw another death for him, and so I saved him from this one."

The Reverend laughed. "You mean God saved him." He looked at her from over the top of the trunk as he took a towel and dried himself off. "You were merely his instrument."

Lily supposed this was true, and so she said nothing to contradict him. Instead, she asked, "Did you know he would live?"

Everyman took up a comb and began smoothing his hair down. "Of course," he told her. "It was all God's plan. Did you see how the people's spirits were lifted up when the boy returned?"

It was true. The crowd, seeing the little boy smiling and wearing his crown of stars, had raised their hands and joined the choir in singing a song called "Washed by the Blood of Jesus." It had ended with the boy, seated on his father's shoulders and waving, leading a procession of worshippers out of the tent and into the night.

Lily was happy to have played a part in whatever plan God had for the boy, but other questions remained. "Can the witch's daughter be saved by baptism?" she asked.

Everyman snorted as he put on a fresh shirt. "Why would you ask such a thing?"

Lily had no good answer for this. "Can she?"

Everyman buttoned his waistcoat. "Do you know that once upon a time, they tested whether or not a woman was a witch by tying her hands and feet and throwing her into water used for baptisms? If she floated, it was because she was touched by the Devil and the holy water was rejecting her. If she sank, she was innocent."

"If she sank, wouldn't she drown?" Lily asked.

The Reverend stepped out from behind the trunk and sat down on a chair. He tugged a sock over one of his feet. "I imagine they pulled her out before that happened."

He still had not answered her question, and so she said, "Have you tried putting the witch's daughter in the tank?"

Everyman, tying his shoe, paused for a moment and looked at Lily. "Why are you so interested in the girl?"

Lily felt her cheeks become warm. "I just wondered if she could be saved."

"Is that all?" the Reverend said, putting on his other sock and shoe.

"I saw her being marked," Lily admitted. She feared saying so would result in trouble, but her curiosity outweighed her worry. "By a man with a machine."

"Ah," said Everyman. "I see. And you want to know why."

"Yes," Lily said. "You said that the marks were made by a devil."

"Did I? I believe I said that the marks were made because her mother consorted with the Devil. Or am I mistaken?"

Lily had several times heard the story about the witch's daughter and her mother. Now she tried to remember exactly what Everyman had said. "I don't recall for certain," she admitted.

The preacher put his hands on his knees. "Sometimes, Lily, people need assistance in understanding their sinful natures. Sometimes, even when given chance after chance to accept God's forgiveness, they refuse because the Devil's hold on them is so great."

"Greater than God?" Lily asked.

Everyman shook his head. "Nothing is greater than God," he told her. "But sometimes God requires us to learn things the hard way, so that we don't forget what he's trying to teach us. Take yourself, for instance."

"Me?" said Lily.

The Reverend nodded. "Have you thought that perhaps what's happened to you is because your father took your mother away from him?"

Lily hesitated in replying.

"Yes, your mother has told me about the godless place he came from, and that he took her there against her will."

At first, Lily thought that he must be lying. Her mother had told her never to speak of the village to anyone. But how else would he know about it if she hadn't told him herself?

"Have you thought that perhaps what happened to your father, and to you, is because he took your mother there?" the Reverend continued. "And that his death was necessary to bring you here?"

"How would God even know about me?" Lily asked.

Everyman stood. He put a tie around his neck and knotted it. "God knows everything," he said. "All our secrets. All your father's secrets. All *your* secrets. Do you think just because the people of your village don't worship him that he doesn't see them? Do you think they can hide from him? Of course they can't. God sees them. And he saw you, and knew that you had to be saved. And so he arranged for it to happen."

"My father loved my mother," Lily said. "And he loved me."

"He may have thought he did," said the Reverend. "But he tried to hide you from God, didn't he?"

"Perhaps he never even knew about God," said Lily.

Everyman finished arranging his tie. "Your mother tried to tell him," he said. "But he wouldn't listen. That's why God had to make other arrangements."

Lily didn't want to hear any more. What the preacher was saying about her father was not true.

"I know it must be difficult to accept." Everyman came toward her, started to put his hand on her shoulder, then pulled it away. "But it's true. And you should thank God for it, because now you have hope. God and your mother, who loved you enough to deliver you out of that place. Don't you agree?"

Lily said nothing. She couldn't bring herself to agree that her father had died because he'd sinned against God. Her father had loved her more than anything. It was the one thing in life of which she was absolutely certain.

"Think how lucky you are," Everyman said. "You could be like the daughter of the witch."

Lily looked into his face. Something about his words felt not like a comfort, but a threat.

"Do you want to be like her?" the Reverend asked. He was no longer smiling.

"No," Lily said.

The smile returned. "I didn't think you did," said the preacher. "Now don't worry about the girl. She's not your concern. Just be happy that the Lord used you tonight. It means you're making progress towards your own salvation."

Lily's heart lightened at this news. But only a little. The preacher's words against her father were still bitter on her tongue. And she would not forget about the witch's daughter. There was more there to understand. But it would have to wait.

"I have business to attend to now," Everyman told her. "And it's time you were in bed. We leave in a few hours."

"All right." Lily left the tent with the preacher. Outside, the air was filled with the sounds of the workmen taking down the rides and loading the trucks. Everyman waved goodbye to Lily as she turned down the road that led to the wagons. She waved back, and walked a little way, until she was certain that he was gone.

Then she turned and went about her real business.

TWENTY TWO

BABA YAGA PLUCKED a crown from the basket and placed it on her head. It fit rather too snugly around her forehead, so she pushed it up until it was perched precariously atop her hair at a jaunty angle. She'd always wanted a crown, and this one was as good as any. Better, really, because if she lost a paper crown, she could just make another one. If it were gold, she would always be worrying about misplacing it, or it being carried off by gnomes.

She climbed the stairs and stood on the edge of the baptism tank, which had yet to be drained. She had not had a bath in who knew how long, and was distrustful of water in general. It was a tricksy thing, too inclined to whimsy for her liking. Also, it was wet.

However, she was intrigued by the notion of baptism. She had overheard the preacher's remarks to the girl about the testing of witches, and had to agree that the principle was sound enough. Now she intended to apply her own rigorous methods to the theory.

She began by dipping her big toe into the tank. When nothing too awful resulted from this initial exploration, she elected to be daring, and leaped into the air with one not-precisely-graceful bend and thrust of the legs. More accurately, she tumbled into the tank in a whirl of arms and legs.

At first, she sank to the bottom. But this was mostly because the water, taken by surprise, was unsure what to do with her. It quickly collected itself, however, and a moment later she was bobbing on the surface. Her crown had slipped off her head and was floating limply beside her.

Well, she thought. *That answers that question.*

Floating was not an altogether unpleasant sensation, however, and so she remained there for a little while, wondering if this was what it felt like to be a mermaid. She imagined luring a sailor into the depth with a song. She tried to think of one.

"In Wellington town at the sign of the plough
There lived a molecatcher, shall I tell you how?
Singing to rel i day fol di lie laddie lie laddie di day"

Her voice creaked and groaned. She practiced batting her eyes and winking coyly.

"He'd go a molecatching from morning to night
And a young fellow came for to play with his wife
Singing to rel i day fol di lie laddie lie laddie di day

"Something, something, oh, bother. I can't remember. Anyway, here's the good bit.

"And while the young fellow was up to his frolics
The molecatcher caught him right fast by his bollocks
Singing to rel i day fol di lie laddie lie laddie di day."

She decided she wasn't really interested in sailors. And she'd had enough of being damp. Somehow, through a combination of flailing and cursing, she managed to get herself to the side of the tank. Dragging herself up the stairs, she stood at the top for a while as the water fled from her. When she was dry, she snatched up another crown and put it on her head.

"Witch or no, I'm keeping this," she announced. She waited for a moment, to see if the preacher's god would try to take it away from her.

"I thought not," she said, pleased to have made her point, even if she was not altogether sure what it was. Then, so he knew for certain she had won the argument, she took a second crown and shoved it into her pocket.

"You can never have too many," she declared as she went off in search of dinner. "To rel i day fol di lie laddie lie laddie di day."

• TWENTY THREE •

FINDING THE GIRL PROVED to be more difficult than Lily had anticipated. She had no idea where the performers lived, and Everyman insisted they remain out of sight when not on stage. Unlike Lily, they were not free to roam about the carnival.

It was Martha, the bearded lady, who told her where to look. Lily found the woman putting a suitcase into the back of one of the trucks. Having looked everywhere she could think of, and finding nothing, Lily ventured to speak to her.

"The girl?" Martha said. "The one he calls the witch's daughter? She rides with the monkeys."

Lily was not fond of the monkeys. There were a dozen of them, small, mangy things that sat on the shoulders of the clowns. They had been trained to hand visitors the paper flowers, and also to carry the collection baskets that were passed around during the services in the big top. They wore tiny hats, and little buttoned trousers to cover their lower halves because otherwise they would continuously stroke themselves in a lewd manner.

"And where are they?" Lily asked Martha.

"The big green truck," Martha said, pointing to one of the vehicles in which equipment was transported. "You'll know by the smell."

She was correct about this. Lily, approaching the truck, found herself trying not to breathe the air around it. It reeked of urine and spoiled food. She couldn't imagine how the witch's daughter could bear it.

There were two small, barred windows on each side of the truck, but they were set high up, and Lily could not look through them. Fortunately, the padlock that secured the rear doors had not yet been closed, and she was able to pull them open. The smell inside was even worse, and it was difficult to see in the dim light.

The monkeys began to screech as soon as the door opened, and the cacophony was disorienting. At first, Lily feared that they were running loose in the truck, and would either attack her or escape through the slightly-open door. Then she realized that they were in a cage built on one side of the truck. There was another cage on the opposite side, and it was in this one that the witch's daughter sat. There was a pile of blankets in one corner, and she was perched on it, her back against the wall and her legs drawn up. She glanced up when Lily entered.

"Shut the door," she said. "They won't be quiet until you do. They think you're here to feed them."

Lily shut the door. The interior of the truck became even darker, and she could see only an outline of the girl in the thin light that came through the windows. But the monkeys at least ceased their racket, although they continued to chatter amongst themselves. Lily saw that their pants had been removed. She avoided looking at them as she walked to the corner where the girl sat.

"What do you want?" the girl asked.

"I saw what they did to you," Lily told her.

"They do a lot of things to me," said the girl.

"The marks," said Lily. "I saw them putting them on you."

The girl touched her skin where the newest marks were. "It's nothing," she said.

"And I heard you ask about your sister," Lily continued.

The girl moved closer to the bars of the cage. "What do you know about her?" she asked.

"Nothing," Lily admitted.

The girl retreated. "The clowns say you're his pet," she said. It sounded like an accusation. "Like one of the monkeys."

"He's helping me," Lily told her.

"Helping you?" the girl said. "The only person he helps is himself. What is he helping you do?"

Lily didn't want to tell her any more. She'd come there because she wanted to do something for the witch's daughter. Now that she was there, she feared she'd made a mistake. She didn't want to tell the girl that she was working toward salvation.

"Was your mother really a witch?" she asked.

"Witches don't exist," the girl snapped.

"Of course they do," Lily said.

"Is that what he told you?" the girl asked.

"No," Lily said.

"Then how do you know?"

Lily started to tell her about the witches she'd known, but quickly realized that she couldn't without revealing too many other things about herself. "I just do," she said.

"You're very good at not answering questions," said the girl. "Something else I imagine you've learned from him."

"Why won't you say his name?" asked Lily.

"Names have power," said the girl. "And I won't give him any by naming him."

"Mine's Lily," Lily told her. She thought perhaps that showing the girl that she trusted her with this knowledge might help. "What can I call you?"

"They call me the witch's daughter, don't they?" the girl said. "You might as well call me that too."

"But it's not your name," Lily said.

"No," the girl agreed. "It's not. And you still haven't told me why you're here."

Lily had no answer for the girl, or at least no answer that would satisfy her. She had only vague feelings: She wanted to help. She wanted to know why. She wanted to understand. But she could put none of these things into words.

"I wanted to see you," she said, knowing this was not really an answer.

Behind her, the monkeys began to shriek.

"Someone's coming," said the witch's daughter. Her voice was tinged with worry, but Lily didn't know for whom.

"I'll go," Lily told her. She backed away from the cage, ignoring the monkeys, who pushed their greedy little hands through the bars and tried to pull her hair.

She opened the doors, peeking through the crack. A clown was walking toward the truck, carrying two buckets. When he set them down momentarily, Lily took the opportunity to slip out of the truck and into the darkness.

The visit with the witch's daughter had not gone as she'd hoped it might. She'd expected the girl to welcome some kindness. She had obviously been ill-treated by the clowns, and Lily suspected she had few, if any, friends amongst the other performers. She couldn't see her talking to Martha, for instance, and certainly not to Edward, the man with no mouth. Did she have only the monkeys for company? Lily couldn't imagine such an existence. Their constant gabbling would drive her mad.

While she'd been in the truck talking to the girl, the clowns had begun taking down the big top. It now lay on the ground, the canvas pooled like a murky lake. Soon it would be rolled up and stored in one of the trucks, and the Holy Gospel Caravan would be on the way to the next location. Lily wanted to go in search of the girl's sister, but she had no time. Her mother would be expecting her back at the wagon.

She made her way there as quickly as she could, skirting the edge of the carnival so as not to encounter too many people. Not that anyone paid any notice to her. They were too occupied breaking down the rides and packing up the bits and pieces that needed to be stored away for the journey. When she arrived at her wagon, however, Lester was already sitting in the truck, smoking a cigarette. He had removed most of his clown makeup, but remnants of it lingered on his neck and around his eyes.

"There you are," he said. "I was just about to leave without you."

"I'm sorry," Lily said. "I was doing something for the Reverend."

Lester grinned. "I bet you were," he said.

Lily, disturbed by his missing teeth and hungry eyes, started for the door of the wagon. "My mother is waiting for me," she said.

"She isn't," Lester said, causing Lily to stop and turn around. He blew a smoke ring through the window. "She won't be stayin' here tonight."

"Where is she?" Lily asked.

Lester drew on the cigarette again. The glow from the burning tobacco lit up his face. "Not here," he said. "But don't worry none. She asked me to look after you."

Lily couldn't imagine where else her mother would be, if not in the wagon. But she didn't dare press Lester for more information. She sensed he was enjoying toying with her, and she didn't want him to think she was upset or worried in any way.

"Why don't you come up here and ride with me for a while," he said. "Keep me company so I don't fall asleep. You wouldn't want me crashin' into anything, would you?"

Getting into the truck with the clown was not something Lily wanted to do. However, it occurred to her that perhaps he could be of some use to her. He might, she thought, know something about the witch's daughter and her sister. So although the idea of sitting beside him repulsed her, she went and opened the truck door.

"That's a good girl," Lester said. "You'll see. It's more fun ridin' up here with me than it is in that wagon alone."

He started the engine, and the truck pulled forward, joining the line of trucks already on the dirt road leading out of the field in which they had been camped. Lily leaned against the door and looked out the open window. It was a hot night, filled with the sounds of crickets and rumbling motors. There was no breeze.

She and Lester rode without speaking, creeping along until they came to a paved road and the trucks could drive more quickly. Lester continued to smoke cigarette after cigarette, and the smell permeated the still air, which despite the open windows seemed trapped in the cab. Lily's throat began to burn, and she wished she could find it in her to ask him to pull over and let her go into the wagon.

"Where are we going?" Lily asked.

"Vinton," said Lester. This meant nothing to Lily, but Lester offered no further information. Besides, one town looked like the next, and she never ventured outside the grounds of the Holy Gospel Caravan anyway.

Lester reached over. Lily flinched.

"Don't get excited," Lester said. "I'm just gettin' something out of the glove box."

He pushed a button, and the box fell open. Inside was a bottle, which Lester pulled out. He uncorked it with his teeth, then took a long pull on it. He held the bottle out to Lily. "Want a swallow?" he asked.

Lily shook her head. Lester placed the bottle between his legs, resting on the seat, and lit another cigarette from the stump of the old one. Lily concentrated on the lights on the truck ahead of them, wondering how long it would take to get to Vinton.

"You and your ma are somethin' of a mystery," Lester said. "Nobody knows much about you. Not even where you're from. It's almost like you're runnin' from somethin'."

Lily looked out the window. Clouds had formed, blotting out the stars, and it felt like rain.

"Let me guess," Lester continued. "Your pa treated her mean."

Lily, thinking of her father's face, and remembering how he had tucked her into her bed each night and kissed her on the forehead, started to object. But maybe it was easier if the man believed what he wanted. Even though it pained her to suggest, even tacitly, that her father had been anything but kind, Lily said, "Yes. That's it."

"I figured so," Lester said. "The way she keeps to herself. Well, mostly," he added as he picked up the bottle and took another drink. "She and the Reverend seem to be gettin' along just fine."

The first drops of rain spattered against the windshield. Lester turned on the wipers, which groaned and slid reluctantly across the glass. They didn't do much to clear away the water, and the view outside became distorted, a kaleidoscope of taillights. It made Lily slightly dizzy. She leaned her head out the window, letting the rain fall on her face.

"Hey," Lester said. "Get your head back in here. You don't want to go getting numoaney."

Lily didn't know what he was talking about, but she did as he asked. She rolled the window up so that the rain couldn't get in, then leaned her cheek against it. She was trying to figure out how to ask Lester about the witch's daughter.

"Must be hard, not havin' many girls your age around," he said. "Must get kind of lonely."

"Sometimes," Lily said, surprised that he would even notice such a thing.

"What you need is a friend. Someone who treats you nice like."

Lily, sensing an opportunity, said, "There's the girl with the marks on her skin."

"The witch girl?" Lester said. He shook his head, as if Lily had spoken a deplorable word. "You don't want to go gettin' mixed up with that one."

"Why not?" Lily asked.

"First of all, the Reverend wouldn't like it none," said Lester. "More important, she's just plain evil."

"Because of what her mother did?" Lily said.

Lester spat out the window. "Just because she is. Some people are born bad."

"Someone told me she has a sister," Lily said.

Lester nodded. "She does," he said. "From what I hear, she's even worse'n the other one. Never seen her myself."

"Why not?" Lily asked.

"They keep her locked up, away from the other freaks," said Lester. "I could see her if I wanted to. Some of the other fellas visit her pretty regular." He looked over at Lily and grinned at her with rotten teeth. "But

I don't want to get messed up with that devilry. I'm a righteous man."

Lily didn't reply to this remark. She was growing tired. The pattering of the rain on the truck's roof and the rhythmic tump-tump-tump of the tires on the road made her want to close her eyes. She did, and soon she slept.

She dreamed about the monkeys. She was in a forest, following a figure who remained just out of her sight. The trees were full of the tiny, mocking figures. As she tried to make her way, they jumped from branch to branch, scolding and hooting in their shrill voices. They sat just above her head, caressing themselves with their tiny hands and reaching for her hair. She tried not to look at them, but they were everywhere.

Then the forest and the monkeys were gone, and she was looking at a disheveled bed in a cramped and dirty room. Lying on the bed, atop a stained and crumpled sheet, was Lester. Several empty bottles were scattered about the floor, and a half-full one was still clutched in his lifeless hand, as if he'd been determined to take it with him to wherever his soul had departed. His head was turned to one side, and a trickle of sick, now dried and covered in flies, ran from his lips onto the pillow.

Lily opened her eyes. Looking down, she saw Lester's hand resting on her leg. He had pushed her dress up, and his grimy fingers were caressing her skin. It was this contact that had triggered the vision of his death.

She still smelled the foulness of the room, still saw his pale, lifeless face as he turned to her and showed his stained smile. "What you need is a friend," he said.

She pushed his hand away and pulled her dress down.

"I was just bein' friendly." He sounded wounded. "Didn't mean nothin' by it. I thought you liked me."

Even though it was still raining, Lily opened the window. She breathed in the clean air, and let the rain touch her face. This time,

Lester didn't tell her to stop.

"Just bein' friendly," he said again.

They didn't speak again. Lily pushed herself as tightly as she could into the corner between the seat and the door. Lester continued to smoke and sip from the bottle. The rain kept falling, and the road rolled on until, with the sun still not up, they turned onto a smaller road and rumbled through fields of corn. When they passed a sign saying WELCOME TO VINTON, Lily began to breathe more easily. And when, twenty minutes later, the truck came to a stop in a field, she leapt out and ran to the wagon. Opening the door, she retreated inside and fell into her bed, where she slept without dreaming.

· TWENTY FOUR ·

"STOP THAT NONsense," Baba Yaga told the monkey, rapping his tiny, busy hand with a stick she'd picked off the floor of the moving truck.

The monkey obeyed, but leaned back, holding on to the bars of the cage with both fingers and toes, exposing himself and daring her not to look. She again smacked him with the stick, this time aiming lower. The monkey yelped and grabbed at himself, which caused him to tumble into a pile of shit-covered straw.

"You think I haven't dealt with that sort of thing before?" Baba Yaga said as he attempted to extricate himself from the mess. "You're lucky I didn't magic it away."

She couldn't really do it, of course, but the monkey didn't know that, and looked alarmed. He wiped bits of straw from his fur and covered himself as best he could. He wished he had his pants.

"Now then," Baba Yaga said. "Tell me about the girl there." She glanced at the other cage, where the witch's daughter was asleep, curled into a tight ball like a kitten.

The monkey chittered an answer, which caused Baba Yaga to raise an eyebrow and snort. "Is that so?" she said. "I'm surprised she allows that. She seems spirited enough."

The monkey scratched himself out of habit, realized what he was doing, and quickly removed his paw. He said something more.

"Ah," said Baba Yaga. "I understand now." She sighed. "I'm beginning to think this world could do with a bit of a sorting out. Which reminds me, what do you think of this god of theirs?"

The monkey, who currently had a finger stuck up his asshole both because he itched back there and because he thought it would keep him from offending Baba Yaga, considered the question. He was seldom asked his thoughts on anything, and had never before had a conversation about subjects much deeper than the wonderfulness of bananas or the unpleasantness of spending most of one's life perched on the shoulder of a clown. He had, however, thought about things on his own, and had developed some firm opinions, which he now shared with the old woman.

"Yes, yes," said Baba Yaga. "I think you're right about that. But religion is such a strange thing, isn't it? Who's to say?"

The monkey elaborated on his previous point. Baba Yaga snorted. "Having your own god is all well and good," she said. "I'm just not sure this one is everything they seem to think he is. I've been waiting for him to turn up, so that I can ask him about some things that have been on my mind, but so far he's kept his distance."

The monkey screeched.

"Yes, I imagine he could be busy," Baba Yaga conceded.

The monkey pointed and said something else.

"Do you like it?" Baba Yaga said. "I could make you one of your own if you like."

She rooted about in her various pockets, pulling out paper and some clever silver stars that she'd discovered could be stuck to things if one licked their backs. After a minute or two of tearing and gluing, she took the tiny crown she'd fashioned and placed it on the monkey's head.

"It suits you," she told him. "Now I suppose the others will think you're their king or some such."

The monkey jabbered.

"Well, it involves a lot of water," Baba Yaga explained. "Yes, I suppose you could do it in a bucket. It didn't take with me, but you might very well have a different result. It might help if you hold them under for a longer time."

The monkey scampered away, calling to his brothers. Baba Yaga left him to his undertaking, opening the back of the truck and scrambling onto the roof, where she could ride with the wind and the rain. As she settled atop the truck, she chuckled to herself as she imagined the clowns' puzzlement when they made their discovery the next morning.

• TWENTY FIVE •

On the Caravan's first night in Vinton, Lily sat in the stands, listening to the Reverend preach. She had met with four visitors earlier in the evening. Their deaths had been difficult ones to witness, but she was becoming used to the seemingly endless parade of violence and sadness. She no longer was shocked. But she was tired. Still, she wanted to see the witch's daughter. She had been thinking about her constantly since their meeting.

As Everyman launched into his now-familiar patter about sin and its consequences, she waited expectantly. The witch's daughter was always the final example, meant to shock anyone in the audience who still doubted the preacher's testimony.

But this time, she didn't appear. Instead, an armless and legless man was brought out in a wheeled chair. The stumps of his truncated limbs looked raw, as if instead of being born with his condition, he had suffered some kind of recent accident. Lily could see that the flesh that remained was held together with black thread that crisscrossed the man's body like the footprints of insects.

Everyman went over to the man and placed a hand on his shoulder. The man winced. Something about his face seemed familiar to Lily.

"My friends," the preacher said. "Tonight I've shown you some tragic examples of the wages of sin. And now, before I offer you the opportunity to come before the Lord and ask his forgiveness, I give you one more. This is Marty. Just weeks ago, he was as whole as I am."

The Reverend stood behind the man's chair and stretched out his own arms, reminding the crowd of what Marty might have looked like with a complete body. He held the pose for a moment before continuing.

"What do you think Marty's sin was, friends?" he asked.

There was a momentary hush. Then a woman shouted out, "Fornication!"

Her enthusiasm encouraged others, and around the tent voices called out: "Blasphemy!" "Sloth!" "Avarice!" In the row just below Lily, a man stood to his feet and bellowed, "Self abuse!"

Everyman let them call out their guesses, cupping a hand to his ear to encourage them to speak more loudly. Whenever a new voice was raised, he pointed a finger in the direction of the speaker and then clapped his hands, suggesting that they might be correct.

"Gluttony!" "Idleness!" "Thievery!"

"Perversion!" "Idolatry!" "Covetousness!"

The Reverend held up his hands. "Thank you, brothers and sisters. You have comported yourselves most righteously. I see that you've studied the word of God and know what it is that most offends him. Yet none of you have guessed correctly."

A disappointed murmur moved through the tent.

"In the book of Matthew," the preacher said. "Jesus says to his disciples, Except ye turn, and become as little children, ye shall in no wise enter into the kingdom of heaven." He indicated Marty. "Many times God offered this man salvation. And many times, this man refused it."

Marty turned his head away. He looked up into the stands, and Lily saw him clearly, and recognized him. He was one of the men who had accompanied Mr. Scratch to the carnival. He had been standing outside the tent on the day on which she had been tested.

"God will only be refused so many times, brothers and sisters!" Everyman continued. "Then there will come a day when he will remind you of his power and might. He reminded Marty of this by making him as a little child again. Now, like a child, he depends on others to feed him, to bathe him, to clothe him. Now, as helpless as a child, he must come before God and ask for forgiveness. Because only then can he be saved."

Everyman walked to the front of the stage, leaving Marty and his chair in the spotlight.

"Come, my friends," he said. "Stand and come forward to receive forgiveness and salvation."

Many in the audience got to their feet, crowding into the aisles to go to the front of the big top, where Everyman and the clowns waited for them. Marty, alone on the stage, watched them with an expression of pain, anger, and humiliation. Lily, recalling the fearless set of his eyes the first time she'd seen him, as if there was nothing in the world stronger than himself, wondered just what had brought him low. Whatever it was, she couldn't see how God would have any part in it.

She left the stands and went out into the night. While the clowns were distracted with their work, she sought out the green truck in which the witch's girl traveled. It was unattended, but the padlock was closed, preventing her from opening the doors.

She found an empty crate and dragged it beneath the window on the girl's side of the truck. Standing on it, she could just barely see through the bars. The witch's daughter was there, sitting in her cage. She was wearing only a thin dress, and they had taken away her blanket. The smell coming from inside the truck was terrible.

"Are you all right?" Lily called.

The witch's daughter looked up at her. "The monkeys are dead," she said. "All but one of them. They say I did it. But I didn't. They were dead when I woke up. They didn't believe me."

"The door is locked," said Lily. "Do you know where the key is?"

"One of the clowns has it. He keeps it on a ring on his belt."

Lily's heart fell. How was she going to find one clown among so many? And once she found him, how was she going to get the key? Still, she wanted to give the witch's daughter hope, and so she said, "I'm going to go look for it."

The girl said nothing in reply, and so Lily climbed down from the crate and left her there as she went in search of the clown. She really had no idea where to begin. The clowns were scattered all across the carnival, some helping with the crowds of worshippers, some operating the rides and attractions, and some simply loitering in the alleyways.

After following half a dozen of them, and finding nothing, Lily was thinking she would have to give up. Then, as she skirted the edge of the midway, she saw Ash. He was on the merry-go-round, sitting astride a painted wooden rabbit that appeared to be leaping through the air. It was blue, and had a saddle decorated with gold and pink roses. Ash was holding onto the pole that extended from its back. As he passed by Lily, he acknowledged her with a nod.

She stood and watched as he circled several more times. Then the music that accompanied the ride slowed, and the carousel came to a stop. Ash dismounted from the rabbit and came over to where Lily stood. He reached into a pocket and held out his palm. On it rested a key.

"How did you know?" she asked, taking it.

"I didn't," Ash told her. "I don't now. But I know you need to open something. This will do that. But only once. Then it will refuse to open anything."

Lily wrapped her hand around the key. "Thank you," she said.

She hurried back to the green truck, pausing only a moment before sliding the key into the padlock. It clicked open, and she pulled it free. Opening the doors, she reeled as a foul odor belched out. She turned her head away, gasping. It was the scent of death.

Fighting the desire to flee, she went inside, covering her nose and mouth with her hand. The witch's daughter was lying on the floor inside her cage, unmoving. Lily rushed to the door and slid the key into the smaller lock holding it shut. She turned it, and it refused to move. Then she remembered Ash's words. She tried again anyway, but could tell it was useless.

"Wake up," she said as loudly as she dared.

The girl stirred. After a moment, she sat up.

Lily glanced about the truck, looking for anything that would help. It was then that she saw the pile of bodies heaped in the other cage. The tiny, furry limbs were tumbled together like sticks. Small, dead eyes stared back at her.

"They left them in here to rot," the witch's daughter said. "To punish me."

"I'll get them out," Lily said.

The girl shook her head. "That will just bring more trouble."

"Then I'll get you out," Lily insisted. "There has to be a way."

Even though she knew it wouldn't work, she began to fumble with the key again. The witch's daughter, reaching through the bars, grabbed her hands. "Don't," she said.

But Lily heard nothing. As soon as their fingers touched, she was enveloped in a vision. What she saw was the witch's daughter as a very old woman. Her hair was white. Her skin was wrinkled. Her eyes were dim and clouded. She was tucked into a bed, looking out of a window towards the sea. There was a storm, but this was all right because the witch's daughter loved storms. And although the old woman could see very little, she was smiling because she was holding the hand of the person she most loved in all the world, and she knew that even though one of them was leaving before the other, one day not so very far off, they would travel through the stars together.

"Don't forget," the witch's daughter said, her voice creaky with age. "No red cord for me."

"No. No red cord. I want to see your ghost at my window."

They laughed together. Then her beloved kissed her. The witch's daughter smiled and closed her eyes. "I think I'll rest for just a minute," she said. She squeezed her beloved's hand. And then she died.

Lily choked back a sob. The room the two women were in was her bedroom in the little house on the cliff. The bed they lay in was hers. And the hand of the witch's daughter's beloved was her hand.

She felt the beloved's heart break, and because it was her own heart, the ache rocked her like a seventh wave. She wanted to let go of the witch's daughter's hand, to stop the pain, but at the same time she wanted to hold it forever. Her fingers tightened on the girl's, and her voice caught in her throat.

"What?" said the witch's daughter, who could not see the future.

Lily could only shake her head. Was what she saw true? She had no reason to believe it wasn't. At the same time, it seemed impossible.

She looked into the witch's daughter's face. For the first time, she saw that the girl's skin was bruised and torn.

"What did they do?" she whispered.

"You can't get me out," the girl said, extricating her hand from Lily's. With the connection broken, Lily felt her heartbeat stumble, then resume its normal pattern. "You need to leave."

Lily wanted to tell her what she'd seen. Perhaps it would give her hope. But how could she tell the girl that they were destined to have a long life together? It seemed ridiculous to even think such a thing, given their circumstances.

"It's going to be all right."

The witch's daughter said nothing. She was trying to breathe the fresh air through the window, but couldn't reach it, even though she stood on her toes.

"It's going to be all right," Lily said again. "I'll be back."

She turned and left the truck. Although it pained her to do it, she fastened the padlock, so that the clowns would not discover her visit. Then she went in search of Ash. Surely once he heard her story, he would help her by making the key so that it would work again.

She found him in the field behind the wagons. He was sitting in the grass, holding a bat to whose leg he was tying something with a piece of string. When he was done, he tossed the creature into the air. It flittered in careless circles about his head, then careened off, zig-zagging across the sky.

"I find them the best way to send messages between worlds," he said to Lily. "Did the key work?"

Lily held out the now-useless key. "Can you magic it again?"

Ash shook his head. "I told you, it works only once. And it wasn't I who magicked it in the first place. Did you waste it?"

"No," Lily said. "But there was a second lock."

"I see. You'll have to open that one on your own."

Lily slipped the key into her pocket. "I saw her death," she said. "The witch's daughter's."

Ash said nothing. He was looking at the moon.

"She grows to be very old." Lily didn't know how to speak about the rest of what she'd seen, as she didn't quite understand it herself.

"That's good, then." Ash lowered his voice. "Assuming she wishes to become old."

"I think she does," said Lily. "She was happy." She paused before adding, "She was loved."

"It's a terrible thing, to be loved." Ash sounded mournful. He turned his head and looked at her. "The clown who holds the keys is drunk and sleeping in the cook tent, behind the sacks of onions."

Lily ran as quickly as she could to the tent, where she found the clown passed out exactly where Ash had said he would be. He was lying on his stomach in the dirt, his head resting on a bag of spilled potatoes, one of which he had apparently tried to eat. His mouth was open, and his snores sounded like water trying to pass through a clogged culvert.

The ring of keys was underneath him, and Lily had to roll him over, ignoring as best she could the vision of his death when she put her hands on him. (He would be killed when another man pushed him out the door of a moving train during a fight over a card game.) She had no idea which key she needed, and so she took the entire ring. It jangled as she hurried back to the truck where the witch's daughter was kept.

She tried several keys before finding the right one, but soon the door to the cage was open. The witch's daughter began to protest, but Lily said, "We can put you back before they even know you're gone."

The girl still hesitated.

"We can look for your sister," Lily said.

A moment later, they were outside the truck. The witch's daughter looked around her uncertainly. "I haven't been outside without one of them guarding me in . . . a long time. I don't even know where to go."

Lily didn't know either. She realized too that they couldn't just walk around the carnival. The witch's daughter would be recognized instantly by anyone connected with the Caravan. It was just a matter of time before they were discovered. Then, she was certain, things would be worse for them both.

"Come with me," she said.

She took the witch's daughter to her wagon. When they got there, the girl looked at it, confused. "My sister is here?"

"No," Lily told her. "But you'll be safe here."

"I don't want to be safe," the witch's daughter cried. "I want my sister!"

"We don't know where she is," Lily said. "And if they catch you, I think you'll never find her."

The witch's daughter looked all around her, as if she might flee.

"Please," Lily said. "You're tired. And hungry."

The girl nodded. "All right," she said. "But just for a short time. Then I have to look for her."

Lily nodded, and opened the door to the wagon. As was usual now, her mother was not inside. Lily stepped inside, then motioned for the witch's daughter to follow her. She lit a lamp, which filled the wagon with a golden glow.

"Sit there," she told the girl, indicating her bed.

The witch's daughter sat, running her fingers over the soft blankets. Lily went to the washstand and poured some water into a bowl. She added some soap and stirred it with a cloth until it formed a lather. Then she carried it over to the bed and set it on the floor. She wet the cloth and touched it to the girl's face. The girl pulled away.

"What are you doing?" she asked.

"It's easier if I do it," Lily said. "I can see where the dirt is."

The girl looked ashamed, but nodded. Lily resumed washing her face, careful not to let her fingers touch the skin. It was difficult to tell where the bruises ended and the marks began, and several times the witch's daughter jerked away when Lily scrubbed too hard. When she was done with the girl's face, she changed the water, throwing the old out the door and refilling the bowl.

"Stand up," she told the girl. "Take off your shift."

The girl stood in the center of the room. She let her dress fall. Lily began washing her, starting at her neck and working down. Neither of them spoke. Thrice Lily emptied and refilled the bowl of water. Each time, it was less dirty than the time before. The fourth time, Lily added no soap.

As she knelt and rinsed the witch's daughter's feet, gently wiping her skin, she realized that the girl had begun to tremble. Looking up, she saw that she was also crying. Her body shook as tears slipped down her face.

Lily stood and, bracing herself for what would come, enfolded the witch's daughter in her arms. The vision of her death came, but to Lily's surprise, it did not sadden her. Instead, she felt only the love that filled the little room at the top of the house on the cliff. It grew and expanded, spilling out of the vision and into the wagon, surrounding both the living and the dead with its warmth.

The witch's daughter held her back, her head resting on Lily's shoulder as her arms wrapped around her and drew her close. The world became a blur, swirling around them in a storm of light and color. Lily felt the other girl's heart beating with her own, and the twin throbbing of them felt like the quaking of the earth. She feared that she might not be able to stand it, and then that it would end.

The witch's daughter lifted her head and looked into Lily's face. Lily saw her both as she was and as she would be, the years racing forward and then retreating, over and over. But whatever her age, the girl radiated beauty.

"My name is Star," she said.

· TWENTY SIX ·

"YOU STOLE MY DEADman's key."

Baba Yaga glared at the changeling. He was sitting on the branch of a spreading oak tree, eating sugared peanuts from a paper bag and swinging his legs.

"Also, your feet are filthy."

"You weren't going to use it anyway," Ash said.

"I was," Baba Yaga objected. "There's this door in a mountain I've had my eye on for several centuries."

Ash sighed. "It probably just leads to a chamber with a princess sleeping inside a crystal coffin. Or a copper egg with a silver egg inside of it and a golden egg inside of that, and finally an enchanted thimble for all your trouble. Something of that sort."

Baba Yaga snorted. "Well, we'll never know now," she said. "And I could use a good thimble. Anyway, how did you get it? Stealing from me isn't easily managed."

"You were asleep," Ash told her.

"I never sleep that soundly—"

"Well, you were drunk," Ash said. "I didn't want to mention it."

"That's more likely." Baba Yaga sighed. "The beer in this world does go to my head."

"The girl needed it more than you did."

"Did she?" said Baba Yaga. "And just what kind of door did she open with it?"

"The most important kind," Ash answered. "One inside herself."

"Pffft," said Baba Yaga. "Now you're just being sentimental."

"Perhaps." The bag of treats crinkled as he dug around for another shell. "Nevertheless, it's true."

"And what did she find?" asked Baba Yaga.

"You don't want to know," said Ash. "You'll say I'm being sentimental again."

"Well, we've already agreed on that point," said Baba Yaga. "Might as well come out with the rest. I'd like to know my key wasn't squandered."

"All right, then," said Ash. "She found love."

Baba Yaga said, "Pffft" again, but more forcefully. "Now you're trying to provoke me."

"Just because you've forgotten what it's like doesn't mean it isn't real," said Ash.

"I haven't forgotten anything," said Baba Yaga crossly. "I simply refuse to believe in things that don't exist."

"Surely you've loved something," Ash said.

Baba Yaga thought about it. "There was a cat I was fond of once. It used to bring me mouse heads."

Ash smirked. "There you are, then."

"So the girl opened this door inside herself and found mouse heads," said Baba Yaga. "That's much better than a magic thimble, I agree." She spit on the ground.

Ash ate some more peanuts. "It's the witch's daughter..." Shells drifted to the ground. "The one she loves."

"Oh? Is that right? Hmm."

"You don't approve?" asked Ash.

"Of course I don't approve," Baba Yaga said. "You know as well as I do what happens when they think they've fallen in love. Pain. Misery. Quests through swamps and briar forests."

"Happiness," said Ash. "Joy."

"You're being contrary," Baba Yaga said. "You know I'm right."

"I don't think either of us is really an expert on the subject," said Ash.

"Well, we don't have human hearts," Baba Yaga conceded. "They're constructed differently. Still, I predict difficulties for them if they insist on persisting with this foolishness."

"How perceptive of you," said Ash.

"Ass," Baba Yaga muttered. "And you owe me something for the key."

"What would you like?" asked Ash.

"I don't know," said Baba Yaga as she walked away. "I'll give it some thought."

"Perhaps I'll make you a love charm," Ash suggested.

Baba Yaga spat, and where her spittle landed, the ground blistered. "Absolutely not. I'd rather have a mouse head."

· TWENTY SEVEN ·

BECAUSE SHE DID not want to bring any more trouble to the witch's daughter, Lily returned Star to her cage. She hated to leave her there, but now that they had found one another, they had hope. And so Lily reluctantly locked the locks and replaced the ring of keys on the still-sleeping clown's belt. She then went back to her wagon and lay awake for the rest of the night, her mind filled with new thoughts and her body tingling with the warmth of love.

The next night, she again found the clown who held the keys passed out, this time behind the truck that carried the prizes for the midway games — the stuffed bears and bottles of Eau de Vie toilet water and collections of edifying verse (*He Walks With Me in the Garden*, penned by the Reverend's maiden aunt, Miss Purity Shorthope) — that the visitors to the carnival could win by tossing balls into milk tins or throwing little hoops around the necks of empty soda pop bottles. Once more she let Star out of her prison, and they spent the remainder of the night together, lying in the grass beneath Lily's wagon and talking until the first faint glow of dawn appeared in the sky and it was time for Star to creep back to the green truck.

Each night Lily waited until the Caravan was mostly asleep, then went in search of the clown. On nights when she couldn't find him, or when he wasn't asleep, she would drag an apple crate to the window of the green truck and talk to Star through the barred window.

In this way, they learned much about one another, but it wasn't until the seventh night that Lily asked again about Star's mother. She had been afraid to, remembering Star's anger the first time Lily had mentioned her, and fearful that it might be something about which she still didn't want to speak. On this night, their first in yet another new town, she had been unable to get the keys, as the clown was engaged in a game of cards with three other men. And so they were talking through the window.

"How did you come to be here?" Lily asked.

Star did not answer right away, and so Lily waited, listening to the new monkeys. To replace the dead ones, the Caravan had acquired a ragtag group of nine ancient, flea-bitten creatures who had spent their entire lives working for a roadside attraction where customers paid a dime to watch the monkeys climb into peach trees and pick fruit, which they then tossed into the bushel baskets held out by the laughing spectators. But the peach trees had recently succumbed to blight, and the now-useless monkeys had been sold to the Reverend for not much more than the cost of a bottle of rye. They were confused by their new circumstances, missed the trees, were afraid of the clowns, and spent all of their time in the cage sadly murmuring to one another.

"My mother had a gift," Star said, making Lily forget the monkeys. Her voice was soft, and Lily could barely hear her. "She told fortunes. Sometimes by looking at palms, sometimes with leaves left in a teacup. But mostly with cards. When our father was alive, she did it in our kitchen, and only as a way to help those who needed their questions answered. She asked for no money, although sometimes when people were grateful they would press her to accept some coins, and she did so that they wouldn't feel they'd gotten something for nothing. But she always gave this money to someone less fortunate than we were. Then our father died, and we became the ones who were less fortunate. My mother had to provide for us. So she began telling fortunes at fairs. Word of her gift spread, and one day the preacher came to see her. He asked her to tell his fortune, and she did."

"What did she see?" Lily asked.

"I don't know," said Star. "But whatever it was, it impressed him. He asked her to join the Caravan. He told her that she could bring us with her. She didn't want to, but he said he would give her more money than she had ever seen before. She told us that she would do it until she had enough for us to live on, then leave. Moth told her not to do it."

"Moth?" Lily said.

"My sister," Star explained. "She has the gift, like my mother. If anything, hers is even stronger. She told my mother not to trust the preacher. She said it would end badly for us. All of us."

"And your mother didn't listen?"

"My mother was very good at seeing the future for other people, but not for herself," said Star. "She thought she could take care of us, and that Moth was worrying too much. But Moth was right."

"What happened?" Lily felt certain she didn't want to know, but she had to ask.

"At first, nothing," said Star. "He treated us all very well. My mother had her own wagon. Moth and I had one too." Star hesitated a moment. "The one you and your mother are in now," she said.

Lily felt her stomach tighten. "Why didn't you tell me?" she asked.

"I wasn't sure at first," Star said. "But then I saw the marks that Moth carved into the wood over the door. They were supposed to keep him out."

"Everyman?" said Lily, already suspecting the answer.

"Sometimes he would come at night," Star explained. "He said it was to make sure we were all right. He would sit on the edge of the bed and read to us from the book. I never liked that, but Moth pretended to be interested because it made him happy."

"Did your mother know he came to you?" asked Lily.

"Not at first," Star answered. "Moth said not to tell her. She had enough to worry about, telling fortunes all day. We didn't want to trouble her. Besides, at first all he did was read. But then one night I woke up because I heard Moth make a sound. When I opened my eyes, he was on top of her. I screamed for him to stop, and he said he was just trying to comfort her because she was having a nightmare. I knew he was lying, but Moth looked so frightened that I didn't say anything. Not then, anyway. But in the morning, I told my mother."

"And what did she do?" Lily asked.

"She went to him." Star's voice turned hard. "She made a deal."

"What kind of deal?"

"He didn't come to our wagon again," Star said. "Instead, he went to hers."

Lily knew something about the ways of men and women. Enough that she understood what Star's mother had done to protect her daughters. But she'd heard the Reverend say many times that such a thing was a sin. Part of her wondered if Star might not be mistaken. But the anger in her words told Lily that she believed what she was saying.

"It was just after the new year when she began to show signs of a baby," said Star. "She hid it as long as she could, but when she started to refuse him, he figured out why. Then he beat her to make her lose it. But she knew how to brew teas and make potions to keep the little one safe. She threatened to curse him if he came near her, to make his manhood shrivel up." Star laughed bitterly. "He believed her, at least long enough for her to have the baby. It was a boy."

"What happened to him?"

"My mother knew it wasn't safe for him in this world. She made another deal. This time with the old ones. She exchanged her child for one of theirs. It was an ugly thing. When the preacher saw it, he accused her of lying with the Devil. When she told him that the child was his and his alone, he struck her. She fell and hit her head. She died two days later."

"Why didn't you and Moth leave then?"

"We were going to," Star said. "But before we could, he took Moth. He's had her ever since. And he told me that if I didn't do as he demanded, he would hurt her."

Now the story was out. Having heard it, Lily was unsure how to feel or think. Star had no reason to lie to her. And it was clear that she believed what she was saying. Yet it was difficult to accept that the Reverend could do what she claimed he had done. She remembered waking up to find Lester's hand on her leg, and the memory sickened her. Was Everyman capable of the same treachery, and worse?

She had many questions, and she could ask Star none of them. The bond between them was still fragile. She feared that testing it would change things irreparably, and that as a result, the vision she saw whenever they touched would change as well. She had not yet told Star what she saw in their joined future. She was afraid that, as Everyman believed, the outcome could be altered if one or both of them made different choices.

This was her great shame: She had not told Star about the curse that was upon her. When asked how she and her mother had come to join the Caravan, Lily had found herself lying. She'd told Star that the Reverend's interest was in her mother, and that the whisperings of the clowns about her own worth to him was simply idle gossip. Star, removed from the larger world of the Caravan, knew no better.

Now the weight of the unspoken truth was becoming difficult to bear. Lily knew that she had to tell Star about herself. She had already revealed as much as she dared, including her life in the village and the death of her father. But she couldn't bring herself to reveal her curse.

She hoped that she would be rid of it soon, and that it would no longer be a problem. Day after day, she was continuing to do God's work. The Reverend was pleased with her. Just that morning he had told her that he sensed a change in her, a step forward on what he assured her was the path to salvation. All she had to do was continue down it.

But if what Star told her was true, then the preacher's word was not inviolable. She didn't want to believe this. Even if she didn't fully understand God, even if she sometimes doubted, she needed to believe that the Reverend was a trustworthy instrument of the Lord.

"We need to find Moth."

Star's words broke through her thoughts, scattering them like leaves.

"Yes," Lily agreed. "I've been looking."

The fact that she could find out nothing about Star's sister worried her. She knew that the girl had to be somewhere in the Caravan. Yet her attempts to locate her all resulted in dead ends. It was frustrating, particularly for Star.

"Can you find some way to ask the preacher?" Star said. "When you're alone with him the next time?"

Lily hadn't the heart to tell Star that she'd tried several times to inquire about Moth. Always she couched it in questions about sin and its consequences, asking the Reverend to recount the story of the witch's daughter more fully. But when he'd suggested that her interest in the girl's fate was unhealthy, she'd stopped.

The clowns were no more useful. All she got from them was leers and cruel laughter. She would have to find another way to discover where Moth was. But now she answered Star's request with, "I'll try."

Star, for her part, had become more docile when dealing with the Reverend and the clowns. Lily had, quite rightly, convinced her that this was the most likely way to get what she wanted, or at least to win a measure of peace. And it was working. Failing to enrage her made her less interesting to them, and now they led her to and from the stage for the daily performances but otherwise left her alone.

"The Reverend is asking for you."

Lily whirled around, startled by the unexpected voice. Behind her, Sims stood with an expression suggesting that he was hardly surprised to find her there. Lily wondered how long he had been there, and whether this was the first time he'd seen her standing on the crate beneath the truck window.

She jumped down. Her heart raced as she waited to be scolded. But Sims said only, "He's in his wagon."

Lily nodded. She feared what would happen to Star once she left, but she had little choice. Now that they'd been found out, refusing to answer the Reverend's summons could only make things worse. Her best chance lay in going to him as quickly as she could and praying that Sims would say nothing.

He didn't follow her as she ran to where Everyman's wagon was parked. As always, it was situated away from the others, in the quietest part of the field where he would not be disturbed. By the time she got there, she was out of breath, and so before knocking she paused on the set of wooden steps that sat in front of his door.

As she waited, she heard a noise, a kind of low moan, as of someone in pain. It grew louder, and was accompanied by angry grunts. Concerned and curious, Lily tried the handle of the door, and found it unlocked. She pulled, and a sliver of the inside of the wagon came into view. She could see a bed, and on it her mother. She saw too the back of the Reverend, who was between her mother's spread legs. He was thrusting back and forth.

Lily knew what she was seeing. Knew too that she was not meant to see it. She very quickly shut the door, turned, and ran away from the wagon. She ran until she escaped the lights of the Caravan and was hidden by the dark, stopping only when she came to a tree whose branches were low enough that she could climb into them. Then she kept climbing, moving higher and higher until she found a place where she could sit, surrounded by leaves, and think about what to do.

Not more than a minute later she heard her name being called. "Lily! Lily, where are you? I know you came this way."

It was her mother. Her voice was shrill with anger. Or was it worry? Lily, terribly afraid of being found, was unsure. She held her breath, fearful that even the slightest rustling of the leaves would betray her hiding spot.

"Lily! Answer me at once!"

Her mother was beneath the tree. Lily shut her eyes and willed her to go away. Her mother carried a lantern, and the light filtered through the leaves as she turned in circles. Lily pulled her feet up in an attempt to make herself even smaller. As she did, one of her shoes caught on a branch and slipped off. It tumbled down through the leaves.

Below her, her mother let out a startled gasp. Then the lantern was raised, and she was peering up into the branches. Lily could see her face illuminated by the light.

"Lily, come down," she said. "I want to talk to you."

Lily shook her head, although her mother could not see this. But she recognized her daughter's silence as refusal, and so tried again.

"If you don't come down, I'll come up," she said. "I'm not so old that I've forgotten how to climb a tree."

She waited until it was clear that Lily wasn't going to do as she'd asked, and then she began to climb. Lily watched, terrified and fascinated, as her mother rose branch by branch into the tree. She would never have thought her capable of it. But there she was, ascending slowly but inexorably through the leaves.

With nowhere to go, Lily pressed herself tightly against the bole of the tree and prepared herself for the inevitable arrival. She had nothing to say to her mother, and didn't want to hear anything her mother might have to say to her. She wanted only to be left alone, to forget what she'd seen and stop thinking about what it might mean. But her mother was determined.

She had been forced to leave the lantern behind, but had hung it on a lower branch so that a bit of light still rose up from beneath her, illuminating her in such a way that her shadow grew to monstrous size. Lily shrank back from the seemingly giant arms and legs that moved, spiderlike, against the scrim of leaves. Her mother reached the branch upon which Lily sat. They faced one another in mute confrontation.

Her mother spoke first. "Lily," she said, using the voice she adopted when she was trying to hide her annoyance. "You're being very disobedient. Don't you remember what the Reverend says about children who refuse to honor their mothers?"

Lily stared at her mother's face. She imagined the moaning sounds escaping from her mouth, which now was set in a tense frown. She pictured her mother's body, now covered by a silk robe, patterned with roses, that Lily had never seen before, and saw it naked and glistening with sweat. She saw the parted thighs, the Reverend pushing between them. She heard once more the grunts and groans, so heated and hungry.

"You're going to come down from here." Her mother's voice was stony. "You're not going to ruin this for me."

Lily covered her ears with her hands. Her mother, seeing this, lost her patience and, forgetting herself, reached out. "Come down at once," she said as her hand began to close around Lily's ankle.

Then she remembered the curse, and her hand retreated.

"It's your father's fault," she said. "He made you think you're something special. Well, look where that got him."

Lily felt her heart catch fire, as if someone had held a match to tinder. Anger flared in her, and before she knew it she had reached out and grabbed her mother's wrist. Her mother tried to snatch her arm away, but Lily's fingers clutched.

"Do you want to know what I see?" Lily asked.

Her mother cried out. "Let me go!"

"Do you want to know?"

Her mother said nothing.

"Leave me alone," Lily said. "Leave me alone, or I'll tell you."

She released her mother's wrist. Her mother hesitated a moment, and then began to descend through the leaves, back the way she'd come. When she reached the bottom, she took the lantern from the branch. Lily waited until the light had retreated fully and she was once again in darkness. Only then did she allow the tears to come.

• TWENTY EIGHT •

"WHY DID YOU DO IT?"

Sims, startled, looked with surprise at Baba Yaga, who seemed to have appeared out of thin air in front of him. Which, in fact, she had. His mind quickly told him that she must have just stepped out from behind a tent.

"Do what?" he asked.

"Tell the girl to go to the preacher's wagon," said Baba Yaga. "I assume you knew what she would find there."

Sims nodded. "I did," he admitted. He didn't know why he was telling the strange old woman his secrets, but somehow he thought it was best not to lie to her.

Baba Yaga cocked her head and squinted her eyes in a manner that had been known to unnerve even the hardiest souls. "Why?"

Sims only shrugged his shoulders.

"Listen," said Baba Yaga. "I enjoy a good plot twist as well as the next person. Probably more. But I like to know the reason. So out with it."

"I'm dying," Sims said.

"So I've heard," said Baba Yaga. "That hardly seems a good reason for giving the girl such a shock. In case you hadn't noticed, she's not as worldly as some."

"I joined the Caravan because I believed God's work was being done here." Sims looked defeated. "I no longer believe that."

"Ah," said Baba Yaga, making connections. "Revenge. The oldest motivation there is. You want to see the preacher fall."

Sims shook his head. "I want to see the girl rise."

Baba Yaga cackled joyously. "Oh-ho! Even better. You want her to be his undoing."

"I want her to see him as he really is," said Sims. "What he makes people become. I thought if she saw him with her mother, it would show her what he is."

Baba Yaga picked her nose and wiped it on her sleeve. "The mother is hardly an unwilling participant."

"True enough," Sims agreed. "But her sins are her own. His are against God."

"You still believe in your god?" asked Baba Yaga. "After everything? Your sickness and all of this?" She indicated the carnival and made a rude gesture.

"I do," said Sims. "He's here. Even now."

"Then why doesn't he do something about it himself? Why leave it to you to accomplish?"

"He created us to do his work," Sims told her. "That's our purpose."

Baba Yaga yawned. "Seems a bit lazy. Then again, none of the gods I've met are much for doing their own laundry or sweeping their own parlors, so I suppose it shouldn't be a surprise that this one is no different."

"I don't understand you," Sims said.

"I don't imagine you do," said Baba Yaga. "I often don't understand myself. Never mind. You'll forget all about me as soon as I'm gone. Now, don't ruin the story for me, but what do you expect the girl will do now?"

Sims sighed. He removed his glasses and rubbed his eyes. "That's up to her. All I can do is show her the truth."

"Well, part of it, anyway," said Baba Yaga. "And as you know, the truth is not often a welcome gift. She could very well refuse it. We'll see about that. What will you do now?"

"Leave," said Sims. "Find somewhere to do God's work until he calls me home."

"To your great reward, I suppose."

"Blessed is the man who remains steadfast under trial, for when he has stood the test he will receive the crown of life, which God has promised to those who love him," Sims said.

"Oh, dear," said Baba Yaga, scraping the inside of her ear and inspecting the blob of wax on her finger. "Not more crowns. That didn't work out terribly well the last time. But have it your way."

She decided that the man was foolish and honest. This was a regrettable combination. Fools could often manage, as long as they kept out of the way, but honest men always made enemies. If he was lucky, the sickness inside him would take him first.

"Well, good luck." Then, because she felt a crumb of regret for the joke she'd played earlier, she added, "You ought to take the monkeys with you. I don't think they're suited for this life. Maybe you can find some peach trees to leave them in. I'm certain that God said he would like that. His will and whatnot."

Sims, bewildered by the encounter, nodded and resumed walking.

He had already packed his suitcase. He had only to retrieve it and walk to the road, where he would wait for someone to give him a ride. God would provide.

By the time he reached his wagon, he had forgotten all about the peculiar old woman.

• T W E N T Y   N I N E •

AFTER THE CONFRONTATION with her mother in the tree, Lily worried that she would be punished for her disobedience. But if her mother told the Reverend about what had happened, he gave no indication of it when next he saw Lily. This occurred a day later, when in the afternoon she was summoned by one of the clowns to appear in his tent. She went anxiously, wondering both what had become of Sims and what would become of her. Coupled with her ongoing fears about Star and Moth, her mind had become a briar patch of worries.

Everyman, however, greeted her as effusively as he ever did. No mention was made of her mother, whom she had not seen since their encounter. Nor did he in any way suggest that he was displeased with her. This relieved her fears somewhat, but she was still cautious. She hadn't forgotten the story Star had told her, and as she listened to the preacher speak, she thought about the fortune teller and her lost child.

"It occurred to me that you must be very lonely here," the Reverend said. "Are you?"

Lily, who had been occupied with wondering how she might ask him about the whereabouts of Moth, realized that an answer was expected from her.

"Lonely?" she said. "No. I have..." Caught off guard, she'd been about to mention that she had someone now. But she couldn't mention Star. "I have you. And God." She wondered if she should list her mother as well, but if the Reverend cared about her absence from the discussion, he said nothing about it.

"Have not I commanded thee? Be strong and of good courage; be not affrighted, neither be thou dismayed: for Jehovah thy God is with thee whithersoever thou goest!" Everyman said. "That's from the prophet Joshua. Have you been reading the book?"

Lily nodded, although truthfully, she had not opened it in a few days.

"Good girl," Everyman said. "And I'm pleased to hear that you think of me as a friend. I *am* your friend. But I think you would like someone closer to your own age, wouldn't you?"

Lily's heart skipped. Was he talking about Star? Trying to trick her into telling him something he already knew? She hesitated.

"Little James," the Reverend called out. "Come in, son."

Lily, confused, looked behind her and saw a boy walk into the tent. Dressed in a white suit that mimicked the one worn by Everyman, he had his yellow hair slicked back in a similar manner as the preacher's. When he came to stand next to the Reverend, it was like looking at father and son.

"Is he yours?" Lily couldn't help but ask.

Everyman laughed. "This is Little James," he told her. "One of the finest preachers I've ever had the pleasure of hearing testify."

The boy grinned. His face was heavy, his neck straining the confines of his collar. Sweat glistened on his cheeks. He lifted his hands and cried out, "Hallelujah, brother Everyman!"

The preacher laughed again. "Hallelujah!" he echoed. "Always filled with the spirit, this boy," he said to Lily. "He's going to be traveling with us from now on."

Lily was uncertain how she was expected to reply to this news. Both the reverend and Little James were looking at her.

"Hallelujah," she tried.

"You can do better than that, sister," Little James said. "After these things I heard as it were a great voice of a great multitude in heaven, saying, Hallelujah; Salvation, and glory, and power, belong to our God." He clapped his hands together and shouted, "Hallelujah!"

"Hallelujah!" shouted Everyman, and Lily pretended to shout along with him.

"You and Little James are going to be good friends," Everyman told Lily. "You'll watch out for one another. And he can instruct you further in the ways of the Lord."

Little James beamed. "That I will, brother. I can tell that sister Lily has a willing heart. I see God working his miracles in her."

"Indeed he is," the Reverend said. "He's placed his hand on her. Now, we have time before the evening service. Why don't you and Lily spend some time together before that?"

"A wonderful idea, brother," Little James said.

The Reverend ushered them to the door, and Little James held back the tent flap as Lily exited into the afternoon sun. He followed, and a moment later, the two of them were walking together. Lily didn't really know what to say or where to go, and so she went in the general direction of the midway.

"How long have you been preaching?" she asked Little James, feeling she should say something.

"Since I started talking. My first word was amen! My parents took me to my first revival when I was two, and I was anointed by the spirit. I gave my first sermon that very night."

"How old are you now?" Lily asked.

Little James stood a bit straighter. "Almost eleven."

"Are your parents here with you?" said Lily.

"Called to heaven," Little James told her. "But that don't matter. I have a heavenly father, and he's all I need."

Lily could tell that she was expected to agree with this sentiment, but she didn't. She missed her father terribly, and always would. Nothing would replace the feeling she got when he held her in his arms, or told her he loved her. She knew this was not how she was supposed to feel, and that she was likely offending God, but she couldn't help it.

"Brother Everyman tells me that your father is in hell," said Little James.

Lily stopped. "He said that?"

Little James nodded. "That's where the unsaved go. He was unsaved, weren't he?"

"He didn't know about God," Lily said. *But he was full of life,* she thought. *And love.*

Little James smiled. "The heavens are telling of the glory of God; and their expanse is declaring the work of His hands. Day to day pours forth speech, and night to night reveals knowledge. There is no speech, nor are there words; their voice is not heard. That's from Psalm 19. What it means is that the very sun and moon tell us that God is real.

Even if we don't know the name of the creator, all we have to do is listen and we'll know he exists. If we don't, that's our own fault."

He continued walking. Lily, feeling as if she had been punched in the stomach, watched him go. After a moment, she forced herself to catch up to him.

"Do you really believe that?" she asked.

"I believe everything the word of God says," said Little James. "If I didn't, I wouldn't be right with the Lord."

"But that's not fair—there should be a second chance for those who have never heard about God."

"And inasmuch as it is appointed for men to die once and after this comes judgment," said Little James. "That's Hebrews. It means you have to decide if you believe while you're still alive. Can't change your mind once you're dead. And like I said, we've all had the chance to know God, even if we don't know him by his name."

It still didn't seem right to Lily. Her father was a good person. His heart was open and he loved and was loved in return. Surely he wasn't doomed to suffer eternal torment just because he'd died without knowing the god of the Reverend and Little James. What kind of god would do that to his creation?

"Are your parents in heaven?" Lily looked up at the sky for a moment.

"My mother is," said Little James. "My father turned his back on the Lord and became a drunkard and a gambler. I imagine he's burning in the lake of fire along with your father. I did my best to bring him to salvation, but I weren't as strong then as I am now."

Lily was horrified to hear the boy talk like this. The worst part was that he sounded so sure of himself. He spoke of these things matter-of-factly, with no emotion except perhaps disappointment in himself for not being able to save his father. That was something Lily understood all too well.

"I was too late with mine," she said.

Little James stopped and turned to her. "I know what you do," he said. "Brother Everyman told me. Let me tell you, we ain't the same. You've got evil in you that needs to come out. I'm filled with the goodness of the Lord. I do his work. You do the Devil's."

"That's not so," Lily argued. "I tell them what I see so they can change their ways."

Little James laughed. "Is that what Brother Everyman told you?" he asked. "Maybe he needs to study his gospel a little more carefully. It is not for you to know times or seasons, which the Father hath set within His own authority. Luke wrote that in the book of Acts. It means only God knows what will happen to us. Here's another one. And I will cut off witchcrafts out of thy hand; and thou shalt have no more soothsayers. How do you like that one?"

He was still smiling, but his eyes were hard now. Lily had no idea what to say. She didn't know the book well enough to quote from it. Nor did she know what most of it meant anyway. All she could do was stare at the boy.

Little James laughed again. There was not an ounce of humor or cheer in it. "Don't look like that," he said. "It ain't your fault. You're just broken. But God can fix you right up again."

Lily found her voice. "Everyone keeps telling me that. But nobody can tell me how."

Little James winked at her. "I can tell you," he said. "But not now. I got to get ready for my sermon tonight. I'll see you later."

He turned and left her standing there amidst the rides and games. She watched him disappear into the crowd. Part of her hated him for what he'd said. But she couldn't help but wonder if he spoke the truth. He'd quoted God's book so easily, and seemed to know what it all meant far better than she did. Even the Reverend didn't quote so freely from it. Maybe the boy was the one who would show her how to escape from the curse she was under.

She went back to her wagon and waited for the nightly service to begin. When she heard the choir singing "This Little Light of Mine," she walked to the big top and went inside, taking a seat in the stands. The crowd was larger than usual, and there was a current of anticipation in the air that she had never sensed before.

"I can't wait to see Little James," she heard a woman say to her friend, who nodded in agreement.

"I saw him in Tuppawany," the first woman continued. "He was so filled with the spirit that he glowed. You'll see."

Lily thought back to the day she had stepped onto the bus coming to the Holy Gospel Caravan. The people there had spoken about Silas Everyman in this way. But this woman sounded even more excited.

The service unfolded as it usually did, with the choir singing and the Reverend working the crowd into a frenzy of spiritual rapture. He brought out Martha, the bearded woman. He showed them the mouthless man and the one with no limbs. And then he brought out Star.

Lily had braced herself for this moment, as she had on every other night that she'd watched from the stands. Whenever Star was on the stage, Lily kept her eyes fixed on her face, willing her to look her way. Lily always sat in the same place, so that Star would know where she was. Even though Star had told her that the lights made it almost impossible for her to see any of the faces in the crowd, Lily tried to will her to turn her head in her direction. And often she did. Then, as the Reverend enumerated Star's alleged transgressions, Lily would sing under her breath a lullaby that her father had sung for her whenever she was sad or unable to sleep.

She did so now.

"Stars above you light the darkness,
shine the way to heart and home.

Follow them 'cross sea and forest,
hear my song and come, love, come."

Her voice was drowned out by those of the Reverend, the choir, and the crowd. But she sang anyway, ignoring the din around her and imagining the words surrounding Star and comforting her.

"In my arms find rest and comfort,
in your bed sleep safe and dream.
Night will pass in hours untroubled,
till you wake at morning's gleam."

Lily sang the words again and again, casting a spell of love around Star that she hoped would shield her from the litany of sins of which she was being accused. She shut her eyes, imagining a circle of warmth and light in which the two of them lay, embracing, unafraid.

The presentation of the witch's daughter was usually the culmination of the service, and as Everyman's by-now-familiar patter came to its end, Lily started to relax. Star's torment was over, at least for the night. And if Lily could acquire the key to her cage, they would spend a few hours together.

But when the Reverend concluded his sermon, no one came to escort Star off the stage. Instead, two clowns wheeled out what appeared to be a box draped with a red cloth. They placed it on the stage beside the preacher, then went and stood behind Star, but did not reach for her as they normally would.

"Brothers and sisters," Everyman said. His voice was solemn, his expression serious. "Earlier, I told you that the girl marked with the Devil's signs was the most unfortunate example of the results of sinning against God you would see before you tonight. But now I confess that I have one greater even than that."

Lily felt the crowd hold its collective breath. Already brought to levels of near-hysteria by the things they had seen and heard, they now wanted to know what could possibly be worse than the demon-marked witch's daughter.

"I hesitated showing this to you," the Reverend continued. "But tonight is a special night. God's power is everywhere. And he has spoken to me and commanded me to show you this."

The Reverend reached out and took a corner of the red cloth in his hand. "As Peter wrote to the churches, Be sober, be watchful: your adversary the Devil, as a roaring lion, walketh about, seeking whom he may devour," he said. "What does that mean, brothers and sisters?" He paused for a long moment. "Demonic possession!" he shouted.

Cries erupted from the assemblage. Everyman held up his hand. "That's right, my friends. The Devil sends his demons to collect souls for him, just as God sends men like me to win them for *his* glory. We're locked in battle every day. And tonight, you're going to witness what happens when one of the Devil's own comes up against a man of God."

He yanked on the cloth, which slid off, revealing a small cage. Inside it was a girl. Her hair was matted, and her skin dirty.

"Moth!"

Lily's eyes found Star as the girl lunged forward. The clowns grabbed her, holding her back. She struggled, hitting out at them and calling out her sister's name. The Reverend glanced at her, then turned back to the audience and shook his head sadly.

"This child is corrupted," he bellowed. "Her soul has been claimed by the Devil, added to his collection. But tonight, we're going to take it back from him. And to help me do this, I have a special guest."

A spotlight found the stage as the choir began to sing. Little James stepped out from between the curtains. The crowd, seeing him, screamed as he walked over to stand beside Everyman.

"Brothers and sisters," the Reverend said, motioning for them to quiet down. "Many of you already know this child of God. You've heard him testify. You've seen the power of the Lord move through him. And tonight you're going to see his greatest work yet. For tonight, he will snatch this girl from the Devil's grasp."

Little James held up his fat, pale hands. He walked to the cage where Moth huddled, pressed against the back. He prowled around it, his lips moving silently, his hands raised up.

"What's he saying?" a man called out.

Little James stopped and turned. "What am I saying, brother?" he said. "I'm telling the demon that it's going to lose. I'm telling it that it's going to need to find another home, because it ain't welcome in this child of God!"

The people cheered. Star, restrained by the clowns, attempted to break free. Lily sat, frozen, as the spectacle unfolded. She knew she could not help, but she had to witness.

Little James thrust his hands through the bars of the cage. The audience gasped. Inside, Moth cowered. She seemed half asleep.

Little James touched her head. "Demon, I command you to come out," he shouted.

"Amen!" cried Everyman.

"Amen!" echoed the crowd.

Nothing happened.

"The demon is strong, brothers and sisters," Everyman said. "It doesn't want to let go. But brother James is stronger!"

"I command you in the name of Jesus Christ, our Lord," Little James shouted. His eyes were shut, and his arms shook, as if a great power passed through him. "And the unclean spirits, whensoever they beheld him, fell down before him, and cried, saying, Thou art the Son of God!" he said.

Moth wilted under his touch. She fell back against the bars. Then she screamed. At the same time, a shadow flew from the cage and through the big top. All around Lily, men and women cried out in fear.

"Don't be afraid," Little James called out. He had come to the front of the stage, where he stood, his finger pointed toward the top of the tent. "It's only the demon fleeing back to hell! Let it go. Let it go back with a message for its master — the Lord will not be mocked! The Lord will seek you out in all your hiding places!"

The crowd clapped as amens and hallelujahs filled the air. Little James stood in the spotlight, Everyman's arm around his shoulder, triumph radiating from him. Lily, though, was looking at Moth. The girl had not moved since uttering the cry. Now two clowns came and silently pulled the wheeled cage back through the curtains. When Lily looked for Star, she saw that she too had been removed.

It was all terribly wrong. Yet nobody seemed to understand this. Lily, alone in her horror, stared at the pandemonium around her and wanted to scream for them to stop. But it was like fighting a whirlwind. All she could do was try to get out before she was caught up in it.

Slipping from her seat, she ran for the exit.

• THIRTY •

BABA YAGA HELD the piece of cloth in front of the lantern concealed just off stage and waved it about. On the canvas wall of the big top a shadow, magnified to enormous size, flapped and fluttered. She drew the cloth quickly away, and the artificial ghost seemed to swoop across the empty space and vanish into the night.

"What a lovely trick," she said, although there was no one to hear her. The big top had emptied hours earlier, and she was alone on the stage.

It had been a wonderful show. She'd watched it all from her perch high above. The new boy was a splendid performer. The girl in the cage too had delivered well, although Baba Yaga suspected that there was nothing rehearsed about her reactions. She had found a very sharp pin, the tip coated in dried blood, lying on the stage beside the place where the wheeled cage had stood. She suspected that were she to inspect the girl's neck carefully, she would find there a tiny hole, no bigger than a spider bite.

It was all typical theatre trickery. She'd seen its like before. (She recalled here a particularly fine version of the story of Long, Broad, and Sharpsight that she'd seen while visiting a distant cousin in Cheb many years ago.) But it was still impressive when it was done well, and the preacher and his boy were admittedly adept at stagecraft.

Still, it was becoming tiresome. That they had some magic in them was undeniable. But it was of a drab, everyday type that didn't interest Baba Yaga terribly much. Although they spoke of gods and devils, their tricks relied on sleight-of-hand and misdirection rather than actual sorcery. True, it took cunning and skill, but it was nothing that any woodcutter couldn't do with a bit of practice.

A selfish woodcutter. One with guile.

They were very good at keeping their audience in a state of belief. The people who came to see them trusted them. That was something. It was easy to gain a crowd's attention, much more difficult to keep it. Yet not only did they keep it, they left the people wanting more.

She wondered if the girl had yet come to see that what had been promised to her was a lie, like the unfortunate goatherd who rescued the Grey King's daughter from the three-headed dwarf and, instead of the chest of gold he'd been promised, was baked into a pie and fed to dogs. Surely she'd realized by now that this god was either dead or uninterested in her affairs. Baba Yaga hoped so, as she had grown uncharacteristically fond of the child, and wanted to see her have, if not a happy life, at least some measure of revenge on those who had done her ill.

Walking to the edge of the stage, she raised her hands and cried, "Hallelujah!" She held the pose for a moment, imagining the echoing roar of hundreds of voices. She could see why it appealed to the preacher and his boy. Having people worship you was heady stuff. She'd seen it often enough in gods and tsars, playwrights and whores. But it only lasted for a time. Then came the inevitable unseating, beheading, descent into obscurity. There were only so many endings a story could have, and the best ones were seldom happy ones.

She wondered what kind this one would have. She suspected she would know soon enough. That was fine with her. She missed her forest, and her chicken-footed cottage. Also, she had a nagging feeling that she'd left a candle burning in her bedroom.

It was time to go home.

• THIRTY ONE •

STAR WAS NOT IN her cage in the green truck. When Lily tried the door and found it unlocked, she hoped for a moment that luck was with her. But when she opened the doors, she saw only the frightened, mumbling monkeys staring back at her. The other cage was empty.

"You're not going to find her."

Little James stepped out of the shadows. The moonlight silvered his hair and made his white suit shimmer. When he smiled, his teeth glistened.

"Where is she?" Lily asked.

Little James licked his lips, though they were already slick with spit. "With her sister," he told her. "Somewhere else." He laughed. "At least they're together."

Lily started to run from him, to go in search of Star and Moth.

"Do you know want to know the truth about Everyman?" Little James called after her.

Lily stopped. She didn't want to give the boy the satisfaction of asking him what he meant by his question, but something in the tone of his voice compelled her to turn and look at him. She waited for him to continue.

"Do you know what he does?" Little James said. "Why he has you read fortunes?"

"So he can help people find salvation. So I can find salvation by helping them."

Little James shook his head. "I don't think you believe that anymore," he said. "Do you?"

Lily didn't reply. After a moment, the boy continued.

"Do you know how much they pay him?" He pointed a manicured finger at her. "For what you see? For what he *tells* them you see?"

Lily didn't know what he was talking about, so she continued to look at him in silence.

"He doesn't give them salvation," said Little James. "He sells it. For a high price. And he don't tell them what you see. Not always, anyway. Not if it's good. He tells them whatever will make them believe they need his help."

Lily found her voice. "Why are you telling me this?"

"You asked me how you could get salvation," said Little James. "You think Everyman is helping you get it. But he ain't. He's taking you farther away from it. But where shall wisdom be found? And where is the place of understanding? Man knoweth not the price thereof; neither is it found in the land of the living. The deep saith, it is not in me; and the sea saith, it is not with me. It cannot be gotten for gold, neither shall silver be weighed for the price thereof."

Lily wanted to tell him that he was lying. But she knew he wasn't. Her heart told her it was true. Everything she'd been feeling, all of the doubts and questions, pointed to this. Only hope had kept her from accepting it. Now hope was gone.

"How can I be saved?" she asked.

Little James shook his head. "You can't," he said. "It's too late for you. You're already dead."

Lily heard in his voice a note of satisfaction, a bit of happiness that he was unable, or unwilling, to disguise. He enjoyed delivering his verdict to her.

She left him there and ran to her wagon. She found the bag she'd stowed beneath the bed, and put some clothes into it. Then she went back into the night. She was going to find Star and Moth, then leave the Caravan together with them. Where she would go, she didn't know. But her place was not here.

As she walked back toward the tents and lights, the bag she carried seem to grow heavier and heavier. She didn't know where to find Moth and Star, nor what to do once she did. All she knew was that she wanted to be as far from her mother, the Reverend, Little James, and the clowns — from the entire Holy Gospel Caravan — as she could get. Yet she didn't know how to get away. Her mother had brought her into this unfamiliar world, and now she was trapped in it.

The morning is wiser than the evening.

The words came to her, spoken in her father's voice. He'd said that to her whenever she was worried and couldn't sleep. And he was right. The things that kept her eyes open while the moon and stars traveled the sky always seemed smaller in the light of the sun. Maybe it would be so now.

Tomorrow the Caravan would travel. Tonight it would sleep. If she could find somewhere to hide herself, she could face the world in the morning. She considered walking as far as she could. But if they came looking for her, that's what they would expect. Better, she thought, to secret herself close by.

She decided on the truck that carried the flowers of salvation. The carnival used thousands of them every week, and they were stored in a truck and shoveled into baskets for the clowns every morning. Lily knew that no one would look in the truck until shortly after dawn, and so she could try to rest there while she waited and formed a plan.

As expected, there was no one around the truck. Lily opened the door and climbed in. The flowers rustled beneath her as she crawled over the mound of them. She went into one of the far corners and made a kind of nest for herself. It felt like lying in a pile of leaves, and reminded Lily of the times she and her father had gathered up fallen leaves and mounded them, then taken turns running and leaping into them and scattering them again.

Thinking of her father, she was overwhelmed by sadness. She missed him, and their life together. She felt farther from home than ever. For this she now blamed her mother. It was not, she realized, the fault of the girl who slept inside of her. She had punished that girl for too long. Now she forgave her, and shifted her anger to where it belonged — first on her mother, then on the Reverend. They had promised her salvation and freedom, but they had given her nothing and taken everything.

She lay there for a long time, holding onto her anger like a blanket. But eventually she grew weary of this, and she fell asleep. And while she slept without dreaming, the girl who lived inside of her awoke and emerged into the world.

When dawn came, Lily opened her eyes and discovered that the roses in which she slept were now red, and that the girl she had tried to keep buried was free. Rather than being frightened by this, she was joyful. She understood the power of blood, especially one's own, and she knew that she had loosed a terrible magic.

"Welcome, sister," she whispered.

Sister.

"I'm sorry I let you sleep so long."

No matter. It only made me stronger.

"This world is not ours. Don't be afraid."

I am not afraid.

"We have work to do."

Let us begin.

Lily gathered up some of the red roses and made a bouquet of them. Another she tucked behind her ear, breathing in its scent and taking strength from it. Then she took up her bag, opened the door of the truck, and stepped out into the new morning. The girl came with her, walking silently beside her.

Her first quest was to find Star. She closed her eyes and tried to sense her beloved's presence. She could feel her heartbeat in the warmth of the sun. She opened up to it and let it fill her until her head throbbed with the sound of it. Then she opened her eyes and walked.

She ignored everyone she passed by, but noticed that they recoiled from her with expressions of fear. It was only then that she looked down and discovered that her dress and legs were stained with the evidence of her sister's passage.

A clown, seeing her, made a face. "Go clean yourself up," he snarled.

Lily held out her bouquet of roses. "The flowers of salvation," she said, and the clown shrank back.

Lily laughed and continued on her way. Her steps were light but filled with purpose as she wound through the midway. It wasn't until she was standing outside the familiar green truck that she realized where her heart had brought her. At first she thought it must be mistaken, but when she opened the doors, she saw that Star was indeed in her cage.

Star, looking up and seeing her, said, "They knew you would come back for me."

"As a dog that returneth to his vomit, so is a fool that repeateth his folly," said the voice of Everyman.

Lily turned around and saw the preacher standing there with her mother on one side and Little James on the other. A trio of clowns stood behind.

"I'm afraid that you're a terrible disappointment," the Reverend said. "To your mother. To me." He looked skyward. "To God."

"The eye that mocketh at his father, and despiseth to obey his mother, the ravens of the valley shall pick it out, and the young eagles shall eat it," said Little James.

"Let her out of the cage," Lily said.

Everyman laughed. "I'm afraid that's not what I had in mind," he said. "I was thinking it might be a better idea if you joined her in there."

Lily's strength faltered as she saw the clowns take a step forward.

Don't be afraid, sister.

Lily met her mother's eyes. "The sickness that takes you has already begun. It's in your blood. Within a year, you will lose your sight. Then who will care for you?" She looked at Everyman. "Not him. Not anyone. You'll die blind and alone."

Her mother put her hand to her mouth and began to sob.

"She's lying," Everyman snapped. "Don't fall for her trickery."

Lily's mother shook her head. "That's how my mother died," she said, her voice choked and filled with fear. "There's no way she could have known that. No one did. Not even my husband."

Lily stepped toward the Reverend. She held out her hand. "Give me the key."

Everyman raised his hand, as if to slap her. But his wrist was caught by someone standing behind him. Someone who had not been there moment before.

"I wouldn't do that if I were you, preacher," said Mr. Scratch.

Mr. Scratch looked very much as he had the last time Lily had encountered him, only larger. Also, his teeth seemed a little sharper, his fingernails a little longer. In his eyes there was a steely glint that had not been so pronounced before, and it was possible that he carried about him a whiff of something charred, as if he had just walked out of a burning house. There was, on his shirt, a stain that might have been an errant drop of strawberry jam, but wasn't.

Everyman, shocked, turned red as he stammered, "Where did you come from?"

"I've come to make a bargain with you," Mr. Scratch said. He released Everyman's wrist and came to stand near Lily. Although she was afraid of the man, Lily didn't move away.

"A bargain?" said the Reverend.

"Yes," said Mr. Scratch. "You know how much I enjoy them."

"What are your terms?" Everyman asked him.

"The girl," said Mr. Scratch. He turned his head and glanced into the truck. "Both girls."

The Reverend fingered the tie at his throat. "And in exchange?" he said.

Mr. Scratch smiled in a way that caused the clowns to step back. "In exchange, I'll give you a choice," he said. "Give me the girls, and I'll give you more money than you would collect in three summers of services. But if you accept it, you abandon your god and leave all this to the boy."

"And if I don't accept?"

"Then you still have your god. And the girls."

Lily watched the Reverend's face. She could see him thinking, weighing, wrestling with himself. The force of his struggle registered in his eyes and in the way his mouth twitched. Sweat sprang forth on his brow.

"The fear of Jehovah is clean, enduring for ever," said Little James in a loud voice. "The ordinances of Jehovah are true, and righteous altogether. More to be desired are they than gold, yea, than much fine gold; sweeter also than honey and the droppings of the honeycomb."

Mr. Scratch walked over and crouched, so that he was looking directly into the boy's face. "Better to reign in Hell than serve in Heaven," he said.

"That ain't scripture," said Little James.

"No, it isn't." Mr. Scratch stood and cracked his neck. "It's something more truthful. Well, preacher? What's your answer?"

Everyman held out a key. "Take them," he said.

Mr. Scratch turned away. "I needed only your answer," he said as he walked into the truck. "Not your key." He touched his hand to the lock on Star's cage and it withered and fell like a rotten apple. He opened the door. "Come, girl," he said.

Star got to her feet and came out. Lily reached for her and took her hand. When Mr. Scratch walked by, they followed him. But as they passed by the Reverend, Mr. Scratch paused.

"One more thing..." He looked at Lily. "Touch him, and tell me how he will die."

Everyman shrank away from them. "That wasn't part of our agreement—"

"Don't tell me my own terms," snapped Mr. Scratch. Then, to Lily, he said, "Go on."

Lily reached out and touched the preacher's hand, which was warm and damp. He struggled to pull it away, but she held it tight. After a moment, she let it go.

Mr. Scratch leaned down. "What did you see?" he asked.

Lily whispered into his ear, the same way she had once whispered into the Reverend's.

"Ah." One of Mr. Scratch's eyebrows rose. "Very fitting, I think."

"What did she see?" the Reverend asked.

"Ask her," said Mr. Scratch.

Everyman didn't look Lily in the face as he said, "Tell me."

Lily shook her head. "I'm done telling. You'll find out for yourself soon enough."

She reached for Star's hand. Star took it, then said, "We're not going without Moth."

Mr. Scratch sighed. "I'm becoming weary of this game. Where is she?" he asked Everyman.

"I don't know where she is," he said. "She ran off last night."

He lies, sister.

The voice of the girl was clear and fierce in Lily's ear.

The clowns know.

"Ask the clowns," Lily said.

Mr. Scratch pointed to the three men standing behind the Reverend. "Where is she?"

None of them answered.

"Four and twenty blackbirds," said Mr. Scratch, and one of the clowns fell to the ground, his mouth agape. The head of a small black bird poked out of it, followed by the rest of the creature, which wiggled its way out, shook its wings, and flew away.

One of the remaining clowns turned and began to run.

"Ashes, ashes, we all fall down," said Mr. Scratch, and the clown tripped, stumbled several steps, and then lay still.

"She's in the tank," the final clown screamed. "In the tank!"

"Thank you," said Mr. Scratch. "Once I met an old man who wouldn't say his prayers, so I took him by his left leg and threw him down the stairs."

The clown's leg buckled, and he screamed, clutching at Everyman. The preacher pushed him away, and the man lurched sideways, falling against Lily's mother. The two of them landed in a heap on the ground, the clown screaming in pain while Lily's mother tried to push him off of her.

Mr. Scratch motioned, the fingers of one hand curling, for Lily and Star to follow him. They did, leaving Everman and Little James to watch their retreating backs.

"Tell me what you saw," Star whispered to Lily. "About the preacher's death."

"Nothing," Lily told her. "I saw nothing. I think the curse is gone."

I took it with me, sister.

Lily squeezed Star's hand. Someday she would explain about the other girl who had live inside of her. Now, though, they had to find Moth.

They went to the big top. The tank for the baptisms was behind the curtain, waiting to be used that night. It was still covered with a tarp. Star ran to it and pulled the cloth away. She let out a cry.

Moth was inside it, just as the clown had said. Her body was unclothed, and she was covered in bruises. A dark necklace of them ringed her narrow throat. Her eyes stared up at Star and Lily, seeing nothing.

Star jumped into the tank and took her sister into her arms. She keened as she rocked back and forth, unable to speak. Lily, familiar with this kind of grief, let her be alone with it. The time for comforting would come later. Right now, Star needed the distraction the pain provided. But then a thought came to Lily.

"Can you give her life?" she asked Mr. Scratch, who was standing some feet away, watching the scene with a curious expression.

He shook his head. "I can only take it."

Lily understood. Magic had its own rules. But her heart was broken anyway. She looked at Star, cradling Moth and stroking her hair as if she could will life back into her, and she saw herself holding her father.

"You should leave," said Mr. Scratch. "There's nothing to be done here."

"Where will we go?" Lily asked.

"That's your choice," said Mr. Scratch. "I've won your freedom, and that's more than I do for most. What becomes of you now is your doing."

Lily turned to thank him, but he was gone. She and Star were alone in the tent. But she knew there were clowns nearby, and without Mr. Scratch to protect them, they were in danger. She went to the tank and touched Star's shoulder. "They'll be coming," she said.

"I can't leave her," Star said. "Not now that I've found her again. Not even for you."

"She won't be alone," said a woman's voice.

The card reader stood near them. The witch. Mother to Star and Moth. Seeing her, Star's tears flowed fresh and hot. The woman nodded at Lily as she passed her, ascended the steps of the tank, and then knelt beside her daughters. She took Star's face in her hands. "Go," she said. "Go with love. I'll take care of her."

Star hesitated another moment. Then she bent and kissed her sister's forehead. Her mother took the tiny body from her. Star embraced them both, then moved toward Lily.

Together, they walked out of the big top and into the morning. They headed for the midway, just coming to life. As they passed the sleepy-eyed men who were setting up the booths and attractions, they began to run. Their feet flew over the grass, moving more and more quickly, carrying them first to the entrance gate, then down the hard dirt road that passed through fields of sunflowers, taking them step by step into a new day.

· THIRTY TWO ·

Baba Yaga gazed at the ghost mother holding her dead child, and found herself experiencing something new: sadness. Or if not sadness, precisely, then at least an appreciation for the mother's loss. It was not a sensation she particularly enjoyed.

This world is getting to me, she thought. *I think I may be in danger of growing a heart.*

The woman stroked her daughter's hair and whispered to her words that Baba Yaga could not hear. But she knew well enough what they were about. Love. Comfort. Sorrow.

She sighed. She'd seen this before, a departed soul whose love for a child (or beloved, or friend, once, memorably, a particularly beautiful diamond-and-ruby choker) was so strong that it allowed her to exist after death when she ought to have passed on to wherever spirits went in their world. It seldom ended well. Love tempered by grief over time turned to rage, and usually someone ended up going mad.

She could see that the mother's strength was fading. It must have taken a great deal for her to remain in this form for as long as she had. Now, with one child dead and the other sent off to an unknown fate, the strain was too much. She was tearing apart, and would be gone soon.

Baba Yaga considered her possible courses of action. Easiest was to leave things to come to their natural conclusion. It was not like her to show interest in, let alone involve herself in, the affairs of other people, unless they had something she wanted, or she was hungry. She had already behaved out of character by following the girl here. Why should she further inconvenience herself?

"Damn," she muttered, realizing that she was going to do something she would probably regret. She went to the woman and her child.

"Go," she said to the mother, who even now was flickering out. "I'll take care of the child. You've done well."

The woman mouthed silent thanks, her voice nothing more than a puff of air. Then she looked one last time at her child, and vanished.

Baba Yaga lifted the dead girl and walked with her out of the big top. She walked until she reached the field of yellow flowers. There she paused a moment, whistled a complicated tune, and her mortar dropped from the sky. She placed the girl's body inside of it, then climbed in after.

With a few mumbled words, the mortar lifted up into the air, where it hung, unmoving, as Baba Yaga surveyed the world below her. She gazed for a final time at the Holy Gospel Caravan and all that it contained. It was a strange place, to be sure, more wild and dangerous even than her forest. She didn't care for it, and this annoyed her.

"You could be so much more than you are," she told it.

She gave instructions to the mortar, and it began to fly. Below, the clowns setting up the merry-go-round looked up and marveled at the meteor shooting across the sky. A moment later, when the big top burst into flame, they hesitated only briefly before abandoning their tools and going to watch it burn to the ground.

· THIRTY THREE ·

AT FIRST THERE was only one road, and only one direction in which to walk. But eventually Lily and Star came to a crossroads, and there they had to make a decision.

"Where are we going to go?" Star asked.

Go home, sister.

Lily heard the voice clearly. And she very much wished she could go back to the village. But she had no idea where it was, or how to get there from where they now stood.

Use the gifts our father gave you.

Stepping away from the road, Lily found a secluded spot amidst a group of blackberry bushes. She sat down on the ground and opened her bag. She took out the mirror and the shell that had been her father's birthday presents to her.

She held up the mirror. Her face was reflected back to her, dirt-streaked and sunburned. After a moment, a second face appeared beside it. It was the girl. She resembled Lily, although her eyes were blue instead of brown, and her face was fuller.

Hello, sister.

"Hello," Lily said.

"Who are you talking to?" Star asked.

Lily held the mirror out, so that Star could look into it. "What do you see?"

Star began to cry. At first Lily thought perhaps she'd been frightened by seeing the other girl's reflection. But when she saw Star touching the marks on her face, she remembered. Because of her love, she had forgotten that this was not how Star had always looked.

She took Star in her arms, and told her how beautiful she was. Star's body shook as she wept. Her tears dampened Lily's hair.

"Look again," Lily told her. "Look with me."

They held the mirror in their joined hands, and looked into it together. Lily expected to see the other girl's face between their own, but she wasn't there. Star, staring at her reflection, touched the marks on her face. Lily followed her fingertips with her lips, kissing each of the symbols in turn.

Star sighed. "I used to be pretty."

"Your face is like the night sky," Lily told her. "A sea of stars."

"A sea of monsters." Star handed the mirror back. "I can't look anymore."

Lily took the mirror and tucked it away. She knew it would take time for Star to believe that she was as lovely as the wild winter storms. But that was all right. Lily would be there to remind her every time she needed reminding.

She still had no idea where they were going, however. And so she took the shell and held it to her ear. From inside came the sound of the sea.

Follow it back. All the way back.

Lily understood. Or thought she did. She would listen for the voice of the sea. It was one thing that never changed. Whatever the season, whatever the time, it remained the sea. It had been there before everything, and it would be there after all the rest was gone and forgotten.

They waited until night fell, as Star feared the symbols that marked her would cause trouble for them. Lily agreed, and felt both angry and ashamed that this was so. But she welcomed the rest.

When the sun was down and they could move unwatched by all but the night creatures, they began to walk again. Lily listened for the sea, sometimes holding the shell to her ear when she lost the sound of its voice. Each time, she found it again, and followed.

They grew weary, and hungry, and Lily wished she had thought to bring some food with them. But they had neither that nor money, and so they had to content themselves with the berries they found on the bushes and the water they drank from a stream.

Towards dawn, they found themselves following the rails of a train. When they came to the train itself, unmoving and silent like a sleeping beast, they climbed into an empty boxcar and waited until the train came to life and began to move. Then they sat in the doorway, watching the world roll by, as Lily listened to the shell and waited for the sea to tell them what to do.

Hours later, with night come again and the train passing slowly through a town, the voice of the sea called urgently, telling them to come. They jumped then, rolling in the dust but unhurt. When they got to their feet, Lily saw the words GOOD EATS flashing in the distance. She remembered the restaurant, and knew that they were close.

She remembered too the kindly waitress, and what she had seen of her death. As they passed the restaurant, she almost went inside, to see if she was still there. But she was sure now that there was nothing that could change the things she'd seen, and so she kept walking.

When they came to the place where Lily and her mother had entered this world, Lily stopped and took Star's hand.

"Close your eyes," she said.

She closed hers as well. She held the shell to her ear, and heard the roaring of the sea. She began to walk. After a few paces, the hard road beneath her feet changed to the wood of a bridge. She opened her eyes.

It was late afternoon. Alex Henry was standing at the end of the bridge, holding a basket of eggs.

"I thought you might want something to eat," he said.

Lily ran to him, Star stumbling behind her because Lily had not let go of her hand. Alex Henry embraced them both.

"How did you know?" Lily asked.

"I didn't." Alex Henry laughed. "I only knew that someday you would return to us. I've been waiting here whenever I can."

"How long has it been?"

"Too long," said Alex Henry. "Long enough. No time at all."

Lily turned to Star, to see if she was all right. When she did, she saw that the marks on her body had changed. Gone were the ugly symbols, replaced by tiny stars that were grouped in familiar patterns on her skin. On her cheek, the Golden Fish swam beneath the Ruined Tower. The Great Snake curled around her forearm, and the Seven Crows took flight across her breast. Lily knew that the whole of the sky was imprinted in her skin.

She touched her finger to one of the stars of the Night Spider where it lay just below Star's left eye. Almost imperceptibly, the constellation moved the tiniest bit away. Lily, delighted, realized that as the stars in the sky moved through the hours and seasons, so too would they move across Star's skin, always changing, always reflecting the heavens.

"What is it?" Star asked, seeing in Lily's eyes that something marvelous had occurred.

Lily took the mirror and showed her. Star gasped. Then she laughed. To Lily, it was the sound of her heart opening up.

"You'll have to teach me all their names," Star said.

"We'll put a window in the roof," Lily promised her. She threaded the fingers of her hands through Star's. "So we can watch them from our bed."

"The house is waiting for you," Alex Henry said. "Maude Coldlove has been keeping it clean. And you'll find one of Barl Poincenot's stews on the stove." He handed Lily the basket of eggs. "Come to me tomorrow, the both of you, and tell me your stories."

Lily thanked him. Then she led Star to the house on the cliff. She hesitated a moment before opening the door. Then she went into the kitchen, which was indeed clean and filled with the smell of supper. She and Star sat at the little wooden table and ate until they were no longer hungry. Then Lily showed her their home.

Everything was as she had left it. Her father's shirts hung in the closet in his room. His shoes were under the bed, his comb on the dresser. Lily would leave them there for the usual year and a day. Of her mother there was no sign. This made her sad, but she understood that not all tales had happy endings, and that not all children had mothers who understood them or wished them well.

She saved her room, the room that was now hers and Star's, for last. She let Star enter before her, and watched as her beloved went right to the window and opened it. For a moment, she remembered how their tale would end. But that was many years away. Tonight was the first of thousands they would spend sleeping in one another's arms safe in the bed overlooking the sea.

"It's even bigger than I imagined," Star said, and Lily knew that she had already fallen in love with the sound of the waves.

Later, they bathed together in the big, white tub. Then they walked to the cemetery where Lily's father was buried. They sat beside his grave, and Lily told him of the past weeks. After promising to visit him again soon, she and Star walked down to the beach, and Star touched the sea for the very first time.

"I wish Moth was here to see this," she said as she and Lily stood knee-deep in the waves. She had not spoken of her sister since the day before. Now, the tears came, adding their salt to the sea's.

Lily stood beside her, holding her hand so that Star understood that she would always be there. She knew that this would not be the last time that they witnessed one another's grief. They would take turns remembering their dead. And over time, the pain would become less bitter and more sweet.

"I want you to tell me all about her," Lily said.

Star nodded, and wiped her eyes. "I want to do something for her."

"I have an idea," Lily told her.

After that, they lay in the grass as the sun went down and the moon came up. Lily pointed to the constellations and named them for Star, showing them where they were on her body. When it was dark, she took Star into the garden and she lit a lantern and hung it in the branches of a peach tree. Then she plucked three pieces of fruit, broke them open, and laid them in the grass beneath the glowing lantern. After a moment, the first moth came fluttering around the light. It was joined by another, then another, until the air was filled with the soft flapping of their velvet wings and the peaches were covered with them as they ate and drank.

"She would love this," Star said. "A banquet just for them."

"We'll do it every night until the cold comes," Lily promised. "You can watch them and think of her."

They sat in the garden while Star told Lily stories of her sister. When they grew weary and their eyes began to close, they climbed the stairs and got into the bed, where they held each other close and listened to one another's hearts beat until they couldn't tell one from the other.

Once again Lily dreamed of a forest. This time it was spring, and the birch trees were dressed in green and silver. Birds sang to her as she walked, and foxes and hares showed her the way to the little house on chicken legs. When she arrived there, she walked up to the door and rapped on it. Only then did she remember that she should be afraid.

Baba Yaga opened the door. "So, you've come back," she said. "Why?"

"I'm ready now," Lily told her. "To answer your riddles."

"It's not your birthday," said Baba Yaga.

"No," Lily agreed. "It isn't. But I've come anyway."

Baba Yaga sighed. "Very well," she said. "But the same rules apply as the last time. If you answer incorrectly, I eat you."

"And if I answer correctly?" Lily asked.

"Then I don't," said Baba Yaga. "And perhaps I give you something. Shall we play or not?"

Lily nodded.

"If you protect it too much, it withers," said Baba Yaga. "If you break it, you make it stronger. If you lose it, you gain more than its weight in gold."

Lily took only a moment to answer. She thought of Star, and her father, and Moth. "Your heart," she said.

Baba Yaga snorted. "That was an easy one," she said. "This one is more difficult. "It shines brightest in the darkest darkness. The smallest drop is bigger than the biggest ocean. When you've lost it all, that's when you will find it."

This one took Lily a bit longer. But then she remembered the nights she'd spent in the wagon, when she'd believed she'd lost everything, and how even the faintest glow of the rising sun could lift her spirits again. She thought too about how Star had looked at her when Lily had shown her that she was no longer alone in the world.

"Hope," she said. "It's hope."

"Yes, yes," Baba Yaga said. "Of course it is. Any child could have guessed that. But you've one more to answer. Here you are. I strangle but still draw breath. I drown but still live. I bleed to death but my heart still beats."

Lily thought hard. Several answers came to her, none of them entirely fitting. Baba Yaga watched her. After several minutes, she cleared her throat. "Well?" she said.

"I'm not certain," Lily told her. "It's not a very nice question."

"I'm not a very nice person." Baba Yaga stomped the floorboards. "And I told you that this was no nursery game. Hurry up and give me an answer. On second thought, I'll go put some wood on the oven while you think it over. That way it will be nice and hot when you fail."

"No." Lily did not like the sound of that at all. "I have an answer."

"Then what is it?" When Lily did not immediately answer, Baba Yaga loomed over her. "Time's up!" Her mouth opened hugely, showing every one of her well-worn teeth.

Lily, who really had no answer at all, cried out, "Murderer!"

Swift as a sneeze, Baba Yaga retreated back into the doorway. "Bah."

Lily, confused, waited to be eaten. When she realized this wasn't going to happen, she also realized that she had guessed the answer to the riddle correctly, albeit accidentally. "A murderer," she repeated.

"I suppose you expected a riddle about love," said Baba Yaga. "They always do. Especially since the first two are so horribly easy. But this one is much better, don't you think?"

"It's...a good one," Lily said. She still shook from the fear of almost being devoured, but she felt she should be polite. She suspected Baba Yaga would have no difficulty changing her own rules if she thought she was being insulted.

Baba Yaga seemed annoyed enough as it was. "Now you've guessed them all, damn you, and I have nothing for my supper." A bit of drool escaped the side of her mouth. "I should eat you anyway. Nobody would be any wiser for it."

"I think a chicken would taste better," Lily said quickly. "Or a trout from the stream."

"Why not all three? But never mind that. You look a bit gamey. You'd probably give me indigestion."

Lily nodded her head. "Almost certainly."

Baba Yaga scratched her chin. "I suppose now you'll be wanting your present," she said.

"That's all right," Lily told her. "You don't have to give me anything. I'll just be going."

"You'll stay right where you are. I'll only be a minute."

The old witch went into the house and shut the door. Lily could hear her moving about. Occasionally she swore quite loudly. There were more than a few bangs and clatters. What sounded like an enormous stack of dishes crashed to the floor and shattered. A moment later, the door opened again and Baba Yaga reappeared.

"Here you are," she said, holding out her hand.

Lily reached out and took the proffered object. It was a spoon. She turned it over and examined it. It was a perfectly ordinary one. Not made of silver. Not engraved with scenes of tsars hunting deer, or enameled with flowers, or gilded with precious metals. If anything, it was a bit ugly.

"It's just a spoon," said Baba Yaga. "In case you were wondering. It isn't magic. Well, no more than all spoons are magic. But it doesn't give you an endless bowl of porridge, or dig a hole through the earth all by itself when you command it to, or anything stupid like that. It carries soup to your mouth from a bowl. Or pudding. Or what have you."

Lily slipped the spoon into her pocket. "Thank you. It's very nice."

Baba Yaga stared at her for a moment. "Don't mention it. I wasn't using it. Besides, you already have everything you need. A home. The stars. The sea. Love." Her left eye twitched as she listed this last thing. "But there never seem to be enough spoons."

Lily nodded. She thought about the last time she'd visited the witch's house. How terrified she'd been. How sure that she was not strong enough to survive what was happening to her. So much had changed since then. She'd lost some things and gained more. Now it was time to see what else life would bring.

"Goodbye," she said to Baba Yaga.

"Good riddance. Now shoo. I'm very busy."

Baba Yaga slammed the door shut. Lily turned and walked back the way she had come. She was in no hurry. She knew that Star would be there when she woke from this dream. She knew that they would lie together in the soft feather bed and discover one another's secrets. That she would kiss Star's mouth, and see the constellations travel her body season after season until they both grew old and were ready for the next adventure.

And they did.

• THIRTY FOUR •

ABA YAGA CLOSED the door.

"It really is a magic spoon, isn't it?"

Baba Yaga looked at the girl. Moth, who was sweeping up the remnants of the broken plates, stopped and lifted an eyebrow. "Well?" she said.

"You're very impertinent," said Baba Yaga.

"And you're a terrible liar."

Baba Yaga sniffed. "I'll have you

know that I'm a very accomplished liar. I've told more lies in an afternoon than you've told in your entire life."

"Only because I don't lie," Moth said. "I always tell the truth. Even when people don't want to hear it."

"I've noticed that," said Baba Yaga. "It's an unfortunate character flaw. I suppose you inherited it from your mother."

"Probably," Moth said. "Star got her beauty. I got the rest."

Baba Yaga was wondering if perhaps she'd made a mistake bringing the girl here. Maybe she ought to have left her in the other world. She would be dead there, of course, which would not be ideal for her. But Baba Yaga wasn't sure that she was prepared to have someone else around all the time. Especially someone who didn't seem to be afraid of her. She'd threatened to eat the child, but Moth had merely laughed at her. It was disconcerting.

"So, the spoon... What does it really do?"

"Very well," Baba Yaga said. "I'll tell you. If you use it to stir sugar into your tea, it turns the sugar to poison."

"It does not." Moth had finished with the sweeping, and now was emptying the ashes from the stove. Baba Yaga hoped that the bones she was clearing away would put some fear into her.

"That's a particularly large femur," she remarked.

Moth ignored her. "If I was going to magic a spoon," she said. "I would make it so that whoever eats from it tastes the love that went into the cooking."

"Don't be tiresome," said Baba Yaga.

Moth chuckled. "I'm going to keep asking until you tell me. So you might as well."

"Fine," said Baba Yaga. "That spoon belonged to Olga Nikitichna Kuklachyova."

She waited for the child to be impressed. When Moth only stared at her, she remembered that she was not from a world where that name would mean anything.

"Olga Nikitichna Kuklachyova was a girl from Bogorodsk," she said. "She had a sister who was very pretty but very stupid. I don't remember her name. Anyway, it's not important to the story. The important thing is that this sister used to swim naked in a pond, which as you know is a foolish thing to do because if you are pretty — or even if you are not — the vodyanoy that lives there is likely to fall in love with you and want to marry you."

"What's a vodyanoy?" Moth asked.

"A kind of water monster. He looks like an old man with a frog's face." Baba Yaga grimaced to give her the effect. "Now stop asking questions and listen. The vodyanoy who lived in this pond did fall in love with the foolish sister, and he caught her and carried her to his home underwater. When Olga Nikitichna Kuklachyova realized what had happened, she went to the pond and called to the vodyanoy. She asked if she could make an exchange — her sister in return for something of the vodyanoy's choosing."

"What did he ask for?" said Moth.

"A spoon," said Baba Yaga. "But not just any spoon. He wanted the spoon that the Troll King used when he ate the caviar that came from the magic sturgeon that lives in the River Kem."

"What's caviar?"

"Fish eggs. Now don't interrupt me again. I'm almost done. Olga Nikitichna Kuklachyova agreed to this arrangement, and she went in search of the Troll King. She went through the usual trials and tribulations, so I won't get into it. In the end she found the Troll King and tricked him into giving her the spoon, which she took back to the pond near Bogorodsk and presented to the vodyanoy. Only when he saw it he said, 'Is that all it is? It's not magic. It's not even beautiful. You can keep it, and I will keep your sister.' And so Olga Nikitichna Kuklachyova went home and carried on as best she could, and every night when she ate her supper with the Troll King's spoon, she was reminded that even when you are cunning and brave, you don't always succeed, because life is hard and often unfair."

"And how did you get the spoon?" asked Moth.

"Oh. Well. Olga Nikitichna Kuklachyova gave it to me," Baba Yaga said. "As a housewarming present."

"You mean you ate her," said Moth. "And took it."

Baba Yaga scratched her bony elbow. "Possibly. It was a long time ago. It could have been any number of things. Maybe she lost it. Maybe I stole it. The point is, the spoon has an interesting provenance."

"What's — "

"History," said Baba Yaga. "Now wash those dishes."

"But the girl doesn't know the story of Olga Nikitichna Kuklachyova," Moth said, ignoring the order. "So what good was it giving her the spoon?"

"I liked that spoon," said Baba Yaga without further explanation.

After a moment, Moth nodded. "I think I understand. This isn't about her. It's about you. You like her well enough that you gave her something that means something to you."

"I don't like anybody!"

Moth said nothing. She went to the sink and picked up a dish and a cloth. Dipping the dish into the water, she began to rub. As she cleaned, she hummed happily.

Baba Yaga watched her for a moment. Yes, this child was going to be a problem. She saw too much. Even into corners that Baba Yaga herself did not care to look into. *This is what you get for leaving the forest,* she told herself. *You ought to have stayed home.*

Perhaps this was true. But what was done, was done.

Besides, it was nice to have the help.

ACKNOWLEDGMENTS

This book owes its existence to the following people:

Katherine Gleason, who twenty years ago listened as I described an idea I had and said, "That could be good," then every couple of years asked me, "Whatever happened to that book about the girl?"

Melissa Gwinn, who said, "You really should write that one."

Sharyn November, who said, "I want to know how this ends."

Steve Berman, who said, "Just finish it."

And most especially everyone who supported the completion of the book by contributing to my Indiegogo campaign, then waited patiently for four years while I got it done.

THANK YOU.

ABOUT THE AUTHOR

Michael Thomas Ford is the author of numerous books for both young readers and adults. When he was a child, he suspected that he might be a changeling, and growing older has not convinced him that he was mistaken. He is fond of thunderstorms, dogs, tattoos, horror movies, clowns, tarot cards, crossword puzzles, books, found photographs, coffee, the ocean, and opera. If you want to visit him, you may venture to **www.michaelthomasford.com**.

ABOUT THE ILLUSTRATOR

Staven Andersen is an Indonesian artist whose work has been featured in such titles as *Red Caps* by Steve Berman and Maggie Tiojakin's translation of Kipling's *Just So Stories*.

CPSIA information can be obtained
at www.ICGtesting.com
Printed in the USA
FSOW01n2236140617
35224FS

9 781590 212684